**Ma...
his ...**

He was carrying the necessary—nothing more. What you did in a town like New York, where all kinds of people, good and bad, were crammed into every square foot of space, had to be surgical. It had to be done with small weapons. You couldn't blast the corruption out of New York. You had to cut it out, piece by piece.

So he was carrying his Beretta 93-R, his special version, made to cycle subsonic cartridges, with a suppressor that allowed it to deliver silent death. The Beretta was his scalpel. But if he chanced to need a hatchet, the Desert Eagle, chambered for .44 magnum, was leathered under his left arm. He was wearing his combat blacksuit, the night garb that was the trademark of the Executioner.

There they were, down on the street. They didn't hide from the cops. They didn't hide from anything. Well, that was the height of arrogance.

The Beretta spoke....

MACK BOLAN®

The Executioner

DON PENDLETON'S
THE EXECUTIONER®
FEATURING MACK BOLAN®

DEEP AND SWIFT

A GOLD EAGLE BOOK FROM
WORLDWIDE®

TORONTO • NEW YORK • LONDON • PARIS
AMSTERDAM • STOCKHOLM • HAMBURG
ATHENS • MILAN • TOKYO • SYDNEY

First edition April 1991

ISBN 0-373-61148-X

Special thanks and acknowledgment to
Carl Furst for his contribution to this work.

DEEP AND SWIFT

A man who has to be convinced to act before he acts is *not* a man of action.... You must act as you breathe.

—Georges Clemenceau,
1841–1929

My ideals, my goals, my *mission,* remain forever sharp in my mind. To allow them to fade is not to act, and I must act as long as I draw breath.

—Mack Bolan

To all the U.S. servicemen and servicewomen
stationed in the Middle East

1

Mack Bolan crouched on a rooftop. He was only three floors above the street, but from here, on the Brooklyn side of the East River, he could see all of lower Manhattan laid out before him, glowing against the clouds as if it were burning. The lights in the tall buildings gleamed against the dirty brown of the nighttime horizon. The night was warm. A little rain had fallen earlier, and the pavement was wet, reflecting light. Rainwater stood in vast puddles on the flat rooftop.

New York. The Big Apple. "*Anything* can happen in New York," was the theme of one of the radio news stations. Bolan knew that was right—anything could happen, anything could come down.

As it would in just a little while.

The warrior checked his weapons. He was carrying the necessary, nothing more. His work in a town like New York, where all kinds of people, good and bad, were crammed into every square foot of space, had to be done with surgical precision. It had to be accomplished with small weapons. The corruption couldn't be blasted out of New York. It had to be cut out, piece by piece.

That made it tougher. More dangerous.

So he was carrying his Beretta 93-R—the version made especially for him, designed to cycle subsonic cartridges, with a suppressor and flash hider that allowed it to deliver quick and silent death. The Beretta was his scalpel. But if he

chanced to need a hatchet, the Desert Eagle, chambered for
.44 Magnum, was leathered under his left arm.

He was in his black combat suit, the night suit that was
almost a trademark of the Executioner. But because combat clothes and weapons would catch the eye of the first
person who saw him on the street, he was wearing a black
raincoat over everything.

Down on the street. There they were. They didn't hide
from the police. They didn't hide from anything.

He could make out maybe six of them. Three were very
young, and two couldn't be more than seventeen. More of
their numbers were at the end of the street. If a blue-and-
white—an NYPD patrol car—approached, those sentinels
would give a quiet alarm, and the sellers would retreat into
the shadows for a minute or two, until the blue-and-white
was out of sight.

Right now they weren't retreating. They were doing business, selling.

Five years ago no one had even heard of crack. Now it
was a multibillion-dollar-a-year business—based on an epidemic. Babies were *born* addicted to cocaine, because of the
crack their mothers had used during pregnancy. Viciously
addictive, it trapped its users and squeezed them until they
bled.

It was estimated that the majority of the crimes committed on the streets of New York in some way involved crack—
from murderous fights among competing dealers, to mug-
gings and burglaries committed by addicts to get the money
for their next fix.

Down on the street, too, were the customers, as brazen as
the dealers. Some cruised up in expensive cars and handed
over crisp new cash, fresh from the bank machines, for the
stuff. Some shuffled out of the shadows and offered a few
pathetic rumpled bills. Young people, old, rich, poor. Men,
women and children.

It was like a flea market. An open market on a Brooklyn
street, and the people who lived there or had their busi-

nesses along the street cowered behind their doors, afraid even to call the police.

That was why the Executioner was in the Big Apple. The trade in crack was out of hand all over the city, just the way it was on this street, and he'd been asked to move in and see if he could do anything about it.

So he was taking a look for a start. There had to be a collector. There had to be a supplier and a collector. Sooner or later *the man* would show up. And he was the one Bolan was interested in. He was the one who could lead Bolan back to the next man up the line, and so on. The Executioner had come to the Big Apple to prune the top off the tree.

This tree. The one he saw on the street below.

PERFECTO GARCIA WAS twenty-two years old, and quite a few men worked for him. He called them men, though they were boys. But they worked for him anyway. Right here, on this turf, these blocks in this neighborhood, which they owned.

He did not in fact, call them men or boys. He called them "hombres." What was more important, they lived by a code that they called *la hombría,* the code of manhood. They had learned it on the streets of Bogotá and Cartagena, and they had brought it to America, where, together with their *cocaína,* it was making them rich.

Perfecto himself would leave the street that night with a thousand dollars in his pocket, at the very least. None of his hombres would go home with less than five hundred. The silver-gray BMW parked across the street was *his* car. The seventeen-year-old blond woman-child who sat in it waiting for him was also his.

If anybody doubted it, they would have to answer to what he carried under his loose-fitting silk jacket—a .38 Smith & Wesson revolver with hardly any barrel at all, made to do exactly what he used it for: thrusting it up under a man's ribs and blasting his heart out.

Because Perfecto was a Colombian, and Colombians played by their own rules wherever they went.

The old mustache petes of the Five Families had dared oppose the Colombians and had learned the new rules. If you knocked over a man under the protection of what they called a man of honor, you would be knocked over yourself. Perfecto snorted. If you knocked a Colombian under the protection of the code of *hombría,* you would be killed—likely tortured to death—and so would your wife, your children, your mother, your father, your brother, your sister, your friends. . . .

The Five Families had scrambled out of the way when the Colombians came in to take over the commerce in the white dust—the white dust that was worth so many dollars per ounce that dealers in gold and platinum could not even imagine. The Five Families were pushed aside, into areas like the corrupting of labor unions, the construction industry, the hauling business . . . and so on and so on. Some of them still dipped money out of towel services.

Well, that was okay, Perfecto figured. The mustache petes could have their nickels as long as they didn't try to intrude on the *real* money. And of course that was temporary. If the "hombres" decided they wanted the construction unions, they would take them over, too. Because they were the most fearful sons of bitches on the face of the earth.

MACK BOLAN WOULDN'T HAVE agreed. He didn't think them fearful. He thought they were vicious punks. It was their viciousness he had been asked to come here to fight.

He knew how men like Perfecto thought. Hell, hadn't he faced it, in all kinds of disguises, from year one? There were always certain guys who figured the ordinary rules of mankind didn't apply to them. Whether it was the code of *omertà,* the code of silence that governed the Sicilian Mafia, or somebody's code of *la hombría,* it was the same. For some people, other people's lives didn't count. That was what had turned Mack Bolan into the Executioner—that was what he was dedicated to fight.

The people who had called him in told him to go out and take a look for himself. But he knew it would be pointless to hit them on the street. He had to find what was behind the street.

Yeah. He'd find out. He might have to take it out of one of those sellers down there, and he knew how to get it out. He would watch. He would identify the one he wanted. And he would take that one.

The one who owned the BMW. That was his target. The point for tonight was to grab the one with the BMW.

BUI DANG NHU—known in America as Pete Nhu—viewed the Brooklyn street from a different perspective.

Colombians...not the least bit cultured. Speakers of a strange minor language spoken only by their own kind—not Chinese, or Russian, or English, or even Arabic, or any of the languages of the civilized peoples of the world. Instead it seemed to be a language confined to menial workers. Indeed, Pete Nhu had never met a person of respect or honor who mumbled away in that oddly intonated language called Spanish.

Those who spoke that language counted for nothing. They were scorned by the Americans. And by all the varied immigrant groups who composed the population of the huge metropolis. As someone had said, nothing worth hearing has ever been said in Spanish.

But these Colombians, racially mixed, culturally deprived and linguistically impoverished, had moved into New York and carved out a line of business for themselves.

And now they had the nerve to try to hold it against a people with honor both old and modern. They showed sheer arrogance by trying to hold what was demanded of them by their superiors! Against people who were their superiors in every respect!

The time had come for these inferior little men to stand aside.

And that was why he, Bui Dang Nhu, was there that night.

MACK BOLAN STOOD on the roof. There was no point in crouching. No one down there was paying the least attention.

For men who could be assaulted from a number of directions, the Colombians were not particularly cautious.

That was what Bill Doctorow, better known as Doc, had told him. The Colombian cocaine crowd ruled by terror. They killed anyone who was potentially in their way, and they counted on the fear they induced to protect them.

Doctorow was a narc. He was worried about something. The coke was around, the crack, but heroin had begun to reappear in quantity. That was odd. There were fads in substances, but heroin had got such a bad reputation that it wasn't anymore the powder of choice among any but the down-and-out addicts who shot it in the stench and squalor of public rest rooms.

Even opium had had a comeback of sorts. Doctorow said there were people smoking opium in New York, society types who called it the "classic" substance and smoked languidly in Park Avenue apartments and analyzed their feelings in many-syllabled words.

Yeah. Doctorow said the drug trade had taken on new aspects. And he thought he knew why. There were some new guys on the scene, besides the Colombians.

But first things first. Mack Bolan stared down from the roof where Doc had suggested he could see it all.

He was ready for the next step. He had identified the man in charge. He could make his move any time, and he didn't figure it was any great challenge.

Then he could target somebody higher.

PERFECTO GARCIA GRABBED a wad of bills out of the hands of one of his men. Speaking to him in Spanish, he said, "The white Porsche. Move, man! He's been sitting there five minutes."

"He'd sit there five *days*," said the young man. "Or five years. Or until he dies and his body rots. And so would the girl with him. I've seen her get out and chase a man across the street. Anything to get the stuff."

"They are customers," said Garcia simply. "Go to the man in the white Porsche right away."

The younger man frowned at Garcia for half an instant, then he moved quickly toward the Porsche.

Perfecto Garcia didn't know that he had just spoken his last words. He had been identified by Pete Nhu—who recognized his conspicuous posture and manner—as the leader of the Colombian dealers on that Brooklyn street.

Pete Nhu himself killed Perfecto Garcia, taking him out with a short burst from an M-16. It was simple and easy. The Colombian crack dealer never knew what hit him— never knew that the torrent of steel that tore through his chest and burst his every vital organ and ended his dreams of wealth and power had come from a weapon in the hands of a man far more bitter than he was.

More than that, he never knew what happened to his soldiers and the merchandise they had ready to sell. Nhu's men were methodical killers. They knew warfare, knew how to make an action and get it over fast. Nhu alone fired an automatic weapon. The rest of the Colombians were taken out with pistols, some of them while drawing their own weapons and staring around in confusion, looking for the enemy mowing them down.

Customers shrieked, threw themselves on the pavement and wailed in terror. But the attackers knew their business. Not a single civilian was hit.

Bolan stared down from his rooftop. The little action was so fast that he had no time to interfere, even if he wanted to. A minute and a half after Nhu shot down Garcia, the quick, vicious firefight was over. The Colombians were dead. Not one of the attackers had been hit.

Two minutes after the action began, the street was quiet. Every one of the Colombian crack dealers was dead. *Every one.*

There was no point in Bolan's coming down from the roof. But what had just gone down was a landmark in his investigation.

2

"Just what I figured," said Doctorow. "The damned Colombians, who thought their viciousness was enough to scare off anybody, have been out-vicioused."

They sat together at the counter of an all-night coffee shop in Brooklyn. Bolan still wore his combat clothes, covered by the black raincoat, and did look a little eccentric on such a summer night. Doc Doctorow, the federal narcotics agent, blended into the surroundings more in his jeans, T-shirt and nylon jacket. He was carrying iron under his jacket.

"They knew what they were doing," Bolan remarked. "It was like a military operation. They moved in quietly, took out the leader first, then mopped up the soldiers. Quick. Neat. Efficient."

"You get any kind of look at them?"

Bolan shook his head.

"Well . . . you had the only look, but I'd still make book on their identify. You've seen 'em before."

"Don't play guessing games," said Bolan. "Who you think they were?"

"One of the best things our country has done," Doctorow said, "has been to take in the South Vietnamese refugees, as many as we can. The boat people. The people who put their asses on the line for us twenty and twenty-five years ago. They—"

"Yeah, yeah," said Bolan. "And most of them have turned out to be the kind of people we're lucky to have."

"Hey, ol' buddy," said Doctorow. "Let me tell ya. Down the street from my house is a junior high school. With a football field. Sometimes I leave the house at sunrise, and as I drive away I see an old man out there on that football field, down on his haunches, bending down and straightening up, praying, greeting the sun as it rises. Every morning that old man is out there praying to the sunrise. I don't know what god he prays to, but I like his spirit. But . . . not all of them are like him. We got some others in the process."

"There were some rotten ones in Nam," said Bolan. "Hey, man, I know."

"I know you do. Well . . . if you're a narc in New York these days, you see where the rotten ones went, some of 'em. I'm beginning to come across them. And they're nothing like this town has ever seen before. I mean, hey, you saw it an hour ago. They move in like Cong, armed like soldiers, and they take out whoever. The Colombians thought they were scary fellows. The Vietnamese are scarier yet. By far."

"They make war right in the middle of a city," Bolan acknowledged. "They did it back home, so I guess it shouldn't be any big surprise that they do it here."

"No big surprise to you and me," said Doctorow, "nor to anybody who saw 'em in action back in the days when. But one hell of a big surprise to an Irish cop trying to keep the peace on the streets of New York. And let me tell ya, one hell of a big surprise to the crazy Indians from Colombia who thought they were the toughest guys in town. Ol' buddy, they learned their dirty tricks in a big way. And they've brought 'em with 'em."

"Am I hearing the word?" Bolan asked.

"You're hearing the word," said Doctorow. "That's why you were asked to come to New York. That's why the big Fed called you in and asked you to come. A new war, Mack Bolan. A new war that some people think only you can win."

Bolan blew a loud breath. "Thanks," he said. "You think I really deserve the honor?"

BUI DANG NHU HAD DONE his job. He had dispersed his soldiers. None of them knew where he was going, none of them really knew who he was, and none of them, even if they wanted to, could identify him to the police or to their enemies.

Besides, none of them would dare.

One element of the action he'd found amusing. The seventeen-year-old girl sitting in the BMW had begged for her life... as if he'd had any intention of killing her. He had stood there by the car, looking at her, and he had not been able to restrain himself. No. He had laughed at her.

And he had left her there, sitting in the car, with a spreading dampness on the leather bucket seat. Her hysteria had been funny.

Afterward he had come home to the Manhattan neighborhood where so many of his countrymen had settled, where Italians had lived before, and some Chinese. On a few streets the elders had been able to establish something resembling the old neighborhoods in Saigon.

That meant that things were as much French as Vietnamese. Most of the signs on stores were in French, if they weren't in English. The young kids couldn't speak the old language. Why should they bother to learn it? It was hardly likely they'd ever have occasion to speak it anymore. He himself had forgotten most of it. But French, that was something else again. French was the language of culture, of civilization, and he cherished it as he cherished the memory of the nuns who had taught it to him.

He walked past a *boulangerie*—bakery—and a store where the sign said *Papeterie*—stationer's—which really sold more lottery tickets than stationery or greeting cards.

The bar where he was heading was called Papillon. There was a Papillon Bar in Paris, and there had been a notorious one in Saigon. This one was on a street corner.

Bui Dang Nhu walked into the bar. It was like a Parisian bar, with a zinc-topped counter, where every drink was offered but wine was the specialty. The girls were behind the bar, three of them at this late hour on a Thursday night. And each was like the butterfly for which the place was named: each dressed in a slender silk dress with a slit skirt, one in yellow, one in blue, one in green.

"Ho, Pete," one of them said, calling him by his American nickname.

He smiled and nodded.

"Thirsty, tired, lonely?" she asked.

"All three. But first, where is the honored one?"

She gestured toward a door in the rear.

"Thanks," he said.

He went inside. The honored one was there, with two young men. Bui Dang Nhu bowed to the elder and began his report.

FRANCISCO PARDO STARED from the window of a dark blue Ford van as it cruised through the street and passed the bar the gooks called Papillon. "Gook" was his name for the Vietnamese. Or for the Japanese, Chinese . . . any Oriental. Little yellow bastards.

Tonight they had gone too far. Perfecto Garcia was dead. His men were dead, five of them. This was not to be forgiven. Not ever. The gooks must be punished, and they *would* be punished, according to the code of *la hombría*.

Pardo turned and looked at his own men, huddled on the floor of the van, each busy checking and rechecking his weapon.

The streets were not quite deserted. Very few New York streets ever were. Most of the people wandering along the sidewalks were gooks. There also a few drunks lurching along the curbs. Some kids, maybe Italian. Although Pardo didn't much care who got hurt—anybody unlucky enough or dumb enough to wander into the line of fire—he had come to kill gooks.

He had four Uzis—his own and three more. The driver had a sidearm, a revolver, but no submachine gun. The driver had his work to do; he didn't need a burp gun.

"All right," Pardo said in Spanish to the driver. "You know the plan. Pull up and stop. Don't move until I say move."

The driver nodded and flipped his cigarette into the street. As Francisco Pardo climbed into the rear of the van, the driver circled the block to return to the Papillon.

He brought the van to a stop directly in front of the bar. Two of Pardo's men slid back the heavy side door.

"Now!" Pardo yelled.

Four Uzis spit fire and steel. The door and windows of the Vietnamese bar were blown away in the hot blast.

Slugs ripped through the three fragile-looking butterflies behind the bar. They twisted like crazed puppets under the impact, as if they were doing a lunatic dance, and when finally they went down, they were hardly recognizable as human.

The two men who had been standing in the bar talking to the girls were all but cut in two and collapsed into twisted heaps of bloodied flesh.

The gunners reloaded, and then four streams of slugs shattered the wooden door at the back of the room. Splinters flew in a cloud. As the gunners moved their muzzles from side to side, slugs stitched the plaster on either side of the door, filling the air with dust.

BUI DANG NHU THREW himself at the body of the honored one, knowing it was futile, that the old man was dead. He could feel the old man's blood soaking through both their clothes and wetting his own flesh with its sticky sweetness.

The head of a younger man had exploded in a shower of red. He too was dead, surely.

Bui Dang Nhu could not imagine how he would survive, or why he should be spared by the explosions of bullets that had already killed the honored one and another. As soon as the gunners outside lowered their muzzles . . .

But they didn't. The firing went on, but it was aimed somewhere else.

The other man who had been sitting with the honored one—his name was Ngo Ba Lac, but he was often called Bob Lac—scrambled to his feet. He had a big automatic in his hand, and he lunged into the splintered door, knocking away the last of the wood. His glance at Bui Dang Nhu was enough to stir Nhu, who thrust off the weight of the honored one and clutched at his shoulder holster to pull his Colt King Cobra .357 Magnum revolver.

The scene in the bar was a horror of carnage. A man had crawled a few paces, leaving a trail of blood before he died. Another was doubled over and, propped up by the bar, seemed to sit in a pool of his own fluids. Except for the blood, the three girls behind the bar looked like flowers crushed under a heel.

The scene on the street was even less believable. The gunmen had shot down people at random. Some, unhurt, stood shrieking at the sky, deranged by what they had seen. The van was still on the block, and Lac knelt, took careful aim and loosed a single shot that punched through the back. Then the van swung around the corner and was gone.

Shot down at random . . . No, that wasn't what had happened. Nhu and Lac could see what had happened. As they stood on the street in front of Papillon, it became clear what it meant. Americans had been spared. Vietnamese had been killed.

BOLAN HAD CHANGED out of his black combat suit, into jeans, a T-shirt and a light nylon jacket. The Beretta hung under his arm. The Desert Eagle was in his hotel room.

It was a good idea to be as inconspicuous as possible, since the street was choked with television cameras and cables and lights, and a hundred newspeople were screaming questions at the police who were trying to sort out the mess.

Doctorow showed his identification as an agent of the Drug Enforcement Administration, and the officer at the blue sawhorse barricade didn't ask for identification from the big man with the grim face.

"O'Brien," Doctorow called.

A uniformed NYPD captain turned abruptly, annoyed, then saw who it was and smiled and stuck out his hand. "Doc. Glad to see ya, but is this your beat? Gang wars?"

"When the Colombians and the Vietnamese go to war, it's over the stuff," said Doctorow.

"Yeah," replied O'Brien. He was a beefy, flush-faced Irishman: a career cop, on the force since he was twenty years old. "Second time tonight, y'know. Who's your friend?"

"Meet Mike Belasko," said Doctorow. "He's working with me. Unofficially."

"You vouch for him?"

"One hundred percent."

"Then he's good enough for me," said the captain, extending a hand to Bolan. "You got a license for that piece you have under your jacket?" he asked Bolan.

"Sort of," said Bolan. "You've got sharp eyes, Captain."

"Years of experience," explained O'Brien. "Many years. And it's okay with me, since Doc vouches for you. But that wouldn't cut much ice with most cops. I'd conceal it better, if I was you."

"Thanks," said Bolan.

"What's the deal here?" Doctorow asked.

"Seven dead inside," answered O'Brien. "Five on the street. All Vietnamese. Maybe three or four of 'em had something to do with the trade in narcotics. The rest—" he shrugged "—civilians."

"It's hit the fan, hasn't it?" said Doctorow.

"Papillon," said O'Brien, nodding toward the shattered bar. "Not known as a front, just as a place where 'Namese hang out. The guys that hit it didn't give a *damn* who they killed, so long as they were Vietnamese."

"Columbian tactics," affirmed Doctorow. "Who's surprised?"

"You want to know what bothers me?" asked O'Brien. He glanced at his watch. "It's only just two o'clock. The night ain't over, Doc. The night ain't over."

THE COLOMBIANS WERE NOT concentrated in a neighborhood the way the Vietnamese were. They were found all over town. Some blocks, though, were clearly known as theirs. Their turf was well defined. The block in Brooklyn where Pete Nhu had hit Perfecto Garcia was one of those blocks. A few Colombians lived there. Everyone else was intimidated. Those who could, moved out.

Yeah. The ones who could afford to, moved out when the Colombians took over a block. That meant there were blocks—some especially on the west side of Manhattan—where apartments not occupied by Colombians were vacant.

The problem wasn't so much that the Colombians meant to hurt their neighbors. It was that when war broke out among them, the viciousness was so horrible that innocent people were killed—and not just occasionally, either. At a building on West Ninety-ninth Street, an entire Colombian family, parents, children, grandmother, uncle and a cousin, were shot to death with automatic weapons, and four members of a neighboring black family were killed by the bullets flying through apartment walls. No one was ever arrested in that mass murder. No one dared speak.

Men like Pete Nhu and Bob Lac knew where the Colombians were to be found in concentration. They had made a point of knowing. And the night was not yet over.

"The old one is dead," Nhu told the others at a meeting in a cellar on the Lower East Side. "The honored one. And many others. Killed by these little men who are scorned by the Americans, by everyone. What do we do?" He looked around expectantly, his dark eyes glinting. A tall, slender, hard-muscled man, he had high and prominent cheek-bones. In appearance, he was a typical Viet. He had been eleven years old when the Americans flew away in helicopters, leaving his family to the fury of the Cong.

Ngo Ba Lac, on the other hand, was of Chinese descent. He was shorter than Nhu, and his compact face was distinctly Chinese. He spoke up, calm and collected. "Anyone who saw what happened at Papillon knows what we must do."

"Yes," said Nhu, his face twisting into a mask of anger and hatred. "The spics must be taught . . . *respect!*"

"Where? How?" a man asked.

"The house on 146th Street," Nhu answered.

The honored one had ordered them to identify a place to strike the Colombians, in anticipation of a night just like this.

More than a month ago they had identified the apartment building on West 146th Street. They had done their recon work and laid their plans. It was a brick building, six stories high, and Colombians occupied the twenty-four apartments inside. Nearly all those Colombians, men and women, dealt crack on the streets. Some dealt only in the white powder, cocaine, but most dealt crack. There had been five murders in the building in the past two years, one of them a triple murder—man, wife and infant child.

Also, the Vietnamese were almost certain a Colombian who lived in the building was the man who had murdered a young Vietnamese woman in the Bronx—because she was selling her kind of white powder, heroin, on a block where he sold crack.

The honored one had said, "If ever we have to teach them a hard lesson, teach it there."

Doc Doctorow and Captain Francis O'Brien also knew about the house on 146th Street.

But there were a lot of others, all over town.

"What am I s'posed to do?" the captain lamented. "I can't put a dozen cops around every house they've got."

"This is war," said Doctorow. "Gang war. And if it wasn't for the fact that innocent people are going to get in the way and get killed, you might not care."

"Gang wars may kill off a lot of animals," said Bolan, "but the ones who win the war and survive are then more dangerous than ever."

"By morning," said Captain O'Brien, "the mayor's gonna be leanin' on me about what's happened already tonight. And what can I do to stop it?"

"You prune the tops off the trees," Bolan affirmed. "That's the only way."

"Yeah," said the captain bitterly. "Get the bosses. Try it. An hour after I bust one, he and his lawyer thumb their noses at me on their way out of the station house. Two or three years later they thumb their noses at me again after a jury finds the bum not guilty or a judge gives him probation. I can get a guy a stiffer penalty for parkin' on the wrong side of the street than I can get for dealin' crack."

"I don't want to see the morning papers," said Doctorow.

"Or the television stations," the captain added.

Doc Doctorow knew who Mack Bolan was. Captain O'Brien didn't. Doctorow figured the Executioner would take some heat off the police department. For a while. But probably only after making it worse for a while.

IN THE BUILDING on 146th Street the apartments were cooled by window air-conditioners. In the living rooms men and women who had not yet gone to bed sat watching late-night shows on big color television sets. Some of them were absorbed by tapes playing in their VCRs. They drank wine, nibbled on snacks. They were comfortable. There was money in their business.

There was no crack in the building, no cocaine. None of them used it themselves, and they didn't want it found in their apartments if the narcs ever tried a raid. They picked up their stuff at the *fábricas* where it was produced, or from the wholesalers.

Although Hispanics had acquired a reputation for being passionate lovers, at half past three in the morning, most of the men and women in the building on 146th Street were asleep, sprawled naked over their beds to let the cool air wash over them. Of those still awake, some were living up to their reputations, succumbing to passion on couches, on the floor, and one couple in their kitchen, she with her back to the counter.

In nearly every home two or more children slept. Some were infants, some toddlers. The oldest child was eleven, and he slept happily, anticipating the morning when he would spend some of the twelve hundred dollars he had made that week on a new pair of Reeboks.

PETE NHU WOULD OPERATE the weapon. He had learned to fire automatic weapons as soon as he was old enough to lift them. There were few infantry weapons, from any country, he could not use.

But the one he would now rely on was odd. It was the kind of thing a man had to resort to when he found himself in a country where military weapons had never just lain around to be picked up. The thing was in fact antique, but he had tested it and knew it was effective.

It was called a Piat, and it had been the standard British infantry antitank weapon in World War II. It somewhat resembled an American bazooka or a German Panzerfaust, but it was entirely different in operation, in that the bomb was not a rocket and no blast issued from the rear of the tube when the Piat was fired.

Nhu had determined how it worked. The bomb—the British called it a grenade—was laid in an open trough at the front of the weapon. When the trigger was pulled, a powerful spring drove a steel rod deep into the rear of the bomb and detonated an explosive charge. The explosion drove the bomb off the rod with great force. The bomb weighed about three pounds and was capable of flying about a hundred yards. On impact it would penetrate tank armor—or a brick wall—and explode inside.

Nhu had wanted an M-203 but hadn't been able to get one. A dealer had sold him two Piats with a dozen bombs. He had promised that the Piats would work, and Nhu had informed him that unpleasant things would happen to him if they didn't. He had tested it once, and it had worked damned well. He counted on it to work tonight.

He had brought along only two other men. Both were armed with M-16s. Nhu had a Mini-Uzi, hanging at his back on a nylon strap. They had come in an ordinary car, a Ford, and they parked it two blocks away and walked toward the building on 146th Street.

Nhu was more than a head taller than the other two. He was dressed in a loose black shirt and black pants—something like the black suits the Vietcong had often worn, even though he hated the Cong worse than death. Ngo Ba Lac and the other man wore jeans and T-shirts. They were a little more Americanized than Nhu.

Lights still burned in some of the apartments. It was as the Americans like to say—the Hispanics kept busy all night.

Nhu had rehearsed his men on the drive uptown. What they were going to do was very simple, straightforward and deadly.

The Piat could not be fired standing. The recoil would knock a man over backward. The recoil would also recock the weapon after every shot, but the device had to be cocked by hand for the first shot—and the spring was so strong it took two men to pull on it.

They struggled and grunted and finally got the thing cocked. Nhu dropped to his knees, then sprawled out full-length on the sidewalk opposite the building. He pulled close the canvas bag that contained his bombs. He had eight of them.

Lac watched skeptically as Nhu unfolded the big flat-bottomed stand near the front of the weapon. He watched him mount the first bomb in the trough. Some fifteen inches long, bulgy round on the front, with a detonator sticking out on a spike, the bomb tapered to a thin rear. Finally there was a cylindrical fin. The bomb looked as klutzy as the launcher.

Nhu pressed the shoulder plate firmly to his shoulder. The weapon had to be fired by pulling back hard on the trigger guard with the right hand—to be sure it was hard against the shoulder—then pulling the trigger with two or three fingers of the right hand. He looked up at Lac, nodded and pulled the trigger.

For half a second nothing happened, as the spring drove the long firing-pin deep into the rear of the bomb. Then the launching charge exploded with a bang and a puff of smoke, the Piat kicked Nhu savagely on the shoulder and the bomb flew.

The bomb arced across the street, slammed into the brick wall of the apartment building, broke through and exploded with a flash and roar that blew glass out of half a dozen windows.

Nhu mounted a second bomb. The weapon had cocked itself, and he raised the front a little higher before he pulled the trigger again.

The second bomb went through a window and penetrated deep into the building before it struck anything solid enough to detonate it. The Vietnamese on the street couldn't see the flash of the powerful explosion but only heard it. But more window glass shot into the street and showered to the sidewalk, and the building began to fill with smoke and dust.

The third bomb hit higher, on the brick wall at the top floor. Nhu lowered his aim and fired his fourth shot into the ground floor, center.

People inside the building were screaming. Fire had broken out on the third floor, all the lights went out. The explosions inside the building were doing far more damage than what was visible from outside—blowing down plaster walls and ceilings.

Nhu's shoulder ached, but he mounted another bomb, settled himself to fire and launched his fifth bomb.

LUISA GOYA LAY FACEDOWN on the floor of her kitchen, not sure if she was bleeding to death and not sure if she cared. Carlos was dead; there was no question about that. Before the lights went out and dust filled the air and burned her eyes and throat, she had seen the ceiling fall in the children's bedroom. There had been no sound from the two children. They had been crushed in their beds, she was certain. So it made no difference if she lived or died.

She rose on her hands and knees and tried to crawl just as the building shook with another explosion, and she dropped on her face in the stinking broken plaster.

She was naked. She and Carlos had been playfully making love in the kitchen. Making...making life maybe. Then death had come.

Damn the *cocaína!* Her father had warned her that nothing good would come of it in the end. Damn those horrible gooks!—for she was certain that was who was out there hurling bombs into their building.

She crawled. She was desperate to find air, to breathe air free of choking dust and of the smoke that was coming now, too. She reached the living room. Her dazed mind registered the odd fact that it was not nearly so badly damaged. The bomb that had killed Carlos had exploded in the kitchen, high on the wall. He had been standing. She had been lying on the floor. The sink had stopped the fragments that would have shredded her body the way they had shredded Carlos's.

Another bomb, exploding on the floor above, had made the ceiling fall on the children.

Here in the living room she could see how it had been. There was a hole four hands wide in the front wall, just above the floor. There was another hole in the wall between the living room and kitchen. ¡*Madre de Dios!* The bomb had flown upward! They were being attacked by artillery!

Luisa raised herself to the window and looked down.

They were down there! She could see them, just three men, with some kind of cannon that sat on the sidewalk across the street. And they were done with it. One of them was folding it up to take it away.

She crawled across the living room, and on the table beside the television set she found the little automatic Carlos carried when he went out to deal. Luisa scrambled across the floor to the window. Tears streaming from her eyes, her body shaking with sobs, she fired at the men on the streets the only retaliating shots that would come from the building on 146th Street.

NHU WAS SURPRISED. He had put eight bombs into the building, and—except for some wild firing at the very end—no one had loosed a shot at them. He and his men had fired not one single round from their M-16s or the Mini-Uzi.

They made their way to their car without the least interference or interruption. As they drove in the Ford, they heard the first sirens.

Nhu pulled the car to the curb at Thirty-fifth Street and Fifth Avenue. He walked to a telephone booth and dialed a number he had carried in his pocket all night. The call was answered in the newsroom of the *New York Times*.

"Tell the Colombians," said Nhu. "Tell the world. Do not trifle with the Watchful Hawks."

3

"Vietnamese," Bolan said grimly. "Sure. That's what they call themselves—the Watchful Hawks. The name *Vietnam* means something like that."

He sat with Doc Doctorow in the deserted coffee shop of the hotel where he was staying in New York, a modest place on Seventh Avenue South, where prices weren't what they were a few blocks away. Doc had come in carrying all the morning papers, and they huddled over cups of coffee, reading what the papers had to say and trying to sort through the events of the previous night.

"Would you believe twenty-three dead?" asked Doctorow. "Plus forty-eight injured. Of the dead, eleven were kids."

"The Watchful Hawks," Bolan repeated. "They know how to hate, and they know how to kill. They were taught by masters."

Doctorow pointed at a newspaper story. "The mayor has detached a hundred cops from all other assignments and put them to work on breaking up what he calls the worst gang war since the '30s. The governor is saying he'll send in the National Guard."

"Not what the man in the street is saying on phone-in radio shows this morning," said Bolan. "They're calling in, saying, 'Hey, great! Let the spics and gooks knock each other off.'"

Doctorow raised his coffee cup. "I'd guess we've got our job laid out for us," he said.

Bolan nodded. "Like always," he said.

"DAMNEDEST WEAPON I ever heard of," Captain Francis O'Brien admitted. "The experts say the Brits used it in World War II. Called a Piat, it is the only thing of its kind. They're amazed there could still be one functioning."

"What I want to know is where they got it," Bolan said.

The NYPD captain stared curiously at Bolan for a moment. Doctorow had not told him who the warrior was, but the captain was a shrewd man and the truth was beginning to dawn on him. In any event, he had decided to trust this man, to give him information he wouldn't ordinarily give a civilian, and see what happened.

"I can make a guess," said Captain O'Brien. "We've got arms dealers around. All kinds. But there's a guy over in Jersey City that handles this kind of stuff. Names's July. A tough SOB, Belasko. Operates behind a palace guard. You won't get in to see him easy."

"Give me an address," said Bolan.

NOTHING WAS EASY in the Jersey City neighborhood where Bolan found the address later that morning. The air smelled of industrial chemicals and the stench of uncollected garbage overflowing battered cans. Poverty and squalor left their unmistakable hallmarks on the grim neighborhood.

The address led him to an abandoned service station, with wrecked pumps, a boarded-up facade, a sagging roof, but also a big garage at the rear, where cars and trucks had once been repaired. It wasn't a bad layout for a man doing a lot of dealing in arms, among other things.

Bolan and Doctorow had been briefed on Adolfo Guilliani, better known as Dolfy July. "A mean mother," the briefing detective had said. Guilliani had been a capo for Barbosa until the Barbosa Family was all but wiped out by the Rossi Family, then he had opted for independence and asked the Commission for the right to operate a very specific noncompeting business in Jersey City. The Jersey bosses had accepted the idea, since none of them wanted to go into the business Dolfy July wanted.

He was the armorer for the Five Families, buying hardware from a diversity of sources, and selling it to the soldiers who enforce the code. He dealt with everything, from M-16s and Kalashnikovs, to lethal little burp guns like the Uzis and personal sidearms. He sold explosives, stuff like Octogen and Hexogen, plus simple old-fashioned dynamite and TNT.

People with special needs went to Dolfy July with a lot of money. But it was only fair. His merchandise cost him a lot. Very little of it could be bought over the counter, anywhere, and it had to be stolen, hijacked, smuggled.

Bolan stood on a mean street, staring at the shuttered-looking building where Dolfy July did business. Doctorow had suggested he wait till night. The man had also wanted to come along, but Bolan had turned him down on both ideas.

In the first place, it was a one-man operation, and a guy like Doctorow, brave and smart though he was, could get killed by trying to do what very few men were trained for.

Night? No way. The point was to talk to Dolfy July, and that meant coming when Dolfy was likely to be in.

To the practiced eye, the place betrayed itself. Some of the plywood was broken off the windows, revealing heavy bars. The doors were steel, and the locks would have secured bank vaults.

The cars parked around on the street and in what had been the pump space were also a giveaway. Not such great cars, but untouched. You left a car on one of these streets, it would be stripped in fifteen minutes. Not these. The strippers were afraid to touch them. Streetwise, the kids and addicts who stripped cars walked a wide path around these.

Sweating inside the black nylon jacket, the Israeli blaster hanging under his left arm, the Beretta high and behind on his hip, Bolan watched. The smog-filtered sunlight of noon made his job more difficult and his mind whirled through the possibilities. A probe. Even that could be dangerous. Anybody who hung around on this street would be spotted sooner or later and probably challenged.

So maybe there was the answer. Let a man come out and challenge.

It took about ten minutes. The hardman didn't emerge out of the building but along the street, maybe ordered over the phone. He was a legbreaker, picked probably because he looked just like that—a goon, not too bright but heavy.

He wore a jacket, just as Bolan did, and on a day like this, a man wearing a jacket was concealing something underneath it. He was muscular and broad shouldered—yeah, a legbreaker, a headcrusher.

"Lookin' for somethin', buddy?" the man mumbled.

"Huh?" Bolan asked, playing a game.

"I said, ya lookin' for somethin'? Huh? Lookin' for somethin'? Or what?"

Bolan shrugged. "Public street," he said.

"Oh. Wiseass. It ain't no public street, buddy. So move ass."

Bolan fixed the man with a hard look that stopped him for an instant, but he recovered quickly and nudged Bolan with a shoulder.

"Careful, fatso," Bolan muttered.

The legbreaker swung. It was a serious mistake. Bolan caught the oncoming punch on his right arm, drove his left fist into the attacker's gut, then grabbed the arm that had thrown the punch and twisted it behind.

The man tried to drive a heel down on Bolan's foot, so Bolan settled him by shoving the arm up his back until it dislocated the shoulder.

To give credit to the man, he didn't shriek. He grunted in pain, then moaned, but he didn't yell.

"Your mistake," said Bolan coldly. "That's one. Wanna go for two?"

"I been had before and I'm still alive," said the leg-breaker.

"You wanna stay that way, you're gonna take me in to see Dolfy."

"Oh. Good. I'm for that. That's gonna be *your* mistake. That's where you get yours."

"Maybe," said Bolan. He reached inside the legbreaker's jacket and pulled out a Colt Agent—a .38 Special six-shot revolver with a two-inch barrel, an ugly little man-killer. "So how you getting me in to see Dolfy?"

"Let go the arm, buddy. Let it down. You got my piece. Lemme—"

Bolan released the dislocated arm.

"We'll just go over and open the door," said the leg-breaker. "I got a key."

Bolan nodded. He knew what was coming down. He gave the man a little shove. "You go in front of me."

"Sure."

Bolan could guess what was behind that door. But it was a way to get it open, and he had the advantage of the big man as a shield in front of him—a big man who didn't have the smarts to guess that Bolan knew the drill and would never let him duck aside and take whatever was waiting behind the door.

They crossed the street, and the man spoke up. "Gotta put my hand in my pocket and get the key."

"What you feel in your back is your own pistol," Bolan warned him.

The man had to use his left hand to reach into his right pocket because his right arm hung hurting and useless.

He shoved the key into the lock. As he turned it, Bolan threw an arm around his neck. He pinned the man with a forearm pressed solidly to his throat, then kicked the door. It swung back to reveal the expected setup, but with a small change.

"Hello, Tommy," the Executioner said. "Long time, huh?"

Tomaso Saveria, aka Tommy Savvy, stood a few yards inside the door, an Uzi cradled under his arm, ready to kill the intruder as soon as the legbreaker ducked out of the way. He recognized Bolan, and his face twisted into a sneer of hate.

"You *son of a bitch!*" Saveria snarled.

"Killed any more little girls lately, Tommy?" Bolan asked, his voice hard and implacable.

Saveria, a hitter for the Venutos, had murdered twelve-year-old Emily Schottenstein on orders of the Venuto Family, to make her father understand that the Venutos were tough. Schottenstein had made the Venutos understand that *he* was tough—within a week after the child's death, Rudolfo Venuto died in an immense explosion that leveled his mansion on Staten Island—but the hitter, Saveria, had escaped both Schottenstein and the Executioner.

"Yeah, tough man," said Saveria. He didn't know Bolan's name. "Little girls. And whoever else. And now, finally you—"

"Tommy!" shrieked the legbreaker. "He's no wimp. He's busted my arm. That's why—"

"S'okay, Ollie," said Saveria. "You take orders good. And your last one is to stand still. The slugs'll go through all that lard."

Tommy Savvy seemed to be enjoying his moment of banter with the sweating, terrified legbreaker. What he had said was true. Slugs from that Uzi under his arm would go right through Ollie and into the soldier behind him.

But Tommy was watchful. He was watching for the warrior to reach for iron. He didn't know Mack Bolan had Ollie the legbreaker's Colt in his right hand.

"Cool it and live," Bolan whispered to Ollie.

Then he thrust the Colt Agent through under Ollie's armpit and loosed a .38 slug into Saveria's ribs.

Saveria folded. He simply dropped to his knees and sprawled on his face without raising the muzzle of the Uzi an inch. The pressure generated in his chest by the penetration of the .38 bullet had burst his heart and lungs and he never knew what happened, but the loud explosion of the short-barreled .38 served as an alarm for everybody else in the building.

Yelling. Scrambling. They came from all over.

Bolan threw the legbreaker aside and ducked to his right, into a doorway between what used to be the salesroom and the lube bay of the old gas station. The oncoming gunners weren't timid. The rooms filled with the explosions of pistols, and slugs chipped the walls.

The warrior dropped to his knees and let the gunners know he meant business by loosing two quick shots from the Desert Eagle.

He hit no one, but the authoritative explosions from the muzzle of the big blaster split the air and blew out huge craters in the concrete block outer wall. The gunners knew they had nothing easy to face, and they backed away and began to fire cautiously, hoping to hit the soldier or nick him with ricocheting slugs.

Bolan holstered the blaster and drew the Beretta. He slipped back into the lube bay, hiding himself behind stacked crates.

Maybe they'd got him. They didn't know for sure—which was just how he wanted it. A gunner, then another, eased carefully around the corner and stepped out into the lube bay.

It was an antiquated setup. They had lubricated cars here, not by raising them on lifts, but by driving them over lube pits—long narrow holes in the floor where the workmen climbed down in and worked on the undersides of vehicles. The floor was still slick with oil spilled over many years.

One of the gunners was a blond, heavy man, gleaming with sweat. He stood with his legs wide apart, a Colt .45 gripped in both hands. His Colt was not the classic 1911 model—the fabled officer's sidearm of the U.S. armed forces for seventy-five years—but the compact version recently introduced by Colt. And the fact that the shooter had this weapon was some indication of how Dolfy July armed people. It he armed his kind this well, he was a menace.

The gunner stepped forward a pace. His confidence grew every second. Yeah. He'd knocked off the invader. Or someone had.

Bolan leveled the muzzle of the Beretta 93-R and steadied it on the man's head. He had chambered a subsonic round.

"Got the son of bitch," said another gunman, stepping out beside the blond one.

"Damned right. One of us did."

The silent round from the Beretta split the fat gunner's head. In his last convulsion he threw out his hands, and his handsome Colt fell to the floor, skidded across the oily concrete and dropped into the lube pit.

The other man gasped, then shrieked. He had no idea where the shot had come from, no idea which way to run.

A third man stepped into the lube room. He had seen the first man fall, and he led the way with an Uzi, sweeping it across the room, chopping crates and walls with a stream of 9 mm slugs.

Bolan dropped him with a silent 3-round burst that broke his ribs open and destroyed his heart and lungs.

Now the second man, who had witnessed the deaths of the other two, dropped his revolver to the floor and raised his hands.

Bolan stepped out from behind the crates. "Okay," he said coldly. "Where's Dolfy?"

"Office . . ." the terrified man whispered.

"How many more guns?"

The man glanced around. "You got 'em, mister."

Bolan didn't believe him. Dolfy July would be protected by pros, and pros didn't give up this easily.

"Well, tell you what," said the warrior. "You go up to Dolfy's office and give him this." Bolan handed the man a sharpshooter's medal. "You give him that and tell him I want to see him. Down here. Alone."

The man took the medal in his hand as if he thought it might be red-hot. He glanced at it for a moment, then walked through the lube bay and into the extensive room behind.

Bolan followed a few paces behind.

What he had expected was what he found. The lube bay was stacked with crates. The room behind was stacked with hundreds more. The air was heavy with the smell of Cosmoline. Guns. The room was an armory. And it was also a trap. A gunner could be hiding behind any of those crates.

The man carrying the sharpshooter's medal walked slowly, timidly through the big room, glancing from side to side. *He* knew gunners waited for the tall man to come on into the room, to follow him between crates.

Bolan knew it, too. He'd holstered the silenced Beretta and drawn the blaster again. A little terror here could help. He stayed back in the door, alert, his eyes searching the rows of crates, looking for the movement that would be deadly.

The man carried the medal through a wooden door in the far end of the big room.

After a moment somebody stepped out into the doorway between the office and the crates. He was in his fifties, with a long drawn face, yellowish white hair oiled and neatly combed, rimless eyeglasses, thick lips and crooked teeth. He wore a black polo shirt and gray slacks.

"Hey!" he yelled. "Everybody be cool. I got no war with this guy. I don' want no war with this guy. Hey, guy! Be cool! I'm comin' out to talk to you." And Dolfy July walked out of his office and down the line of crates.

Bolan backed into the lube room. Adolfo Guilliani, Dolfy July, walked through the door and into the room. He frowned over the twisted bodies of his two soldiers, then looked into the grim face of the Executioner.

"Plus Tommy Savvy," Bolan said. "You should check out your help better before you hire them. I don't like guys who kill little girls."

Dolfy July shrugged. "You didn't come to talk to me about my employment problems," he said calmly.

"True. I want you to come with me. I don't trust your guys not to come blasting again."

The gangster shrugged again. "I figure this isn't a bust," he said. "Or a hit. I figure you really do want to talk to me."

"I want to talk to you," Bolan agreed.

"Well, let me tell you somethin', big guy," said Dolfy July. "If you're not the man who's entitled to drop sharp-shooters' medals around, take my advice and don't do it. The guy who *is* entitled don't like it. And I wouldn't cross him. In fact, figurin' you may be that guy, I'm out here talkin' to you. I got no beef with that guy, and I can't think why he'd have any beef with me. So I'm out here, talkin'."

Bolan pointed toward the door, and Guilliani walked out through the salesroom, where the body of Tommy Savvy lay, and on out into the sunlight. Bolan pointed up the street, and they walked away from the abandoned station, along the littered sidewalk.

"So?" asked Guilliani.

"The bomb thrower the Viets used last night on 146th Street," Bolan said.

Dolfy July glanced up into Bolan's face, then gestured with his hand and kept on walking. "What about it?"

"Who'd you sell it to?" Bolan demanded in low tones.

Guilliani turned down the corners of his mouth. "Who says I sold it?"

"I do," said Bolan. "And it may be true that you and I have no beef. It just *may* be. But I want to know who bought the Piat and the bombs it shot into that apartment building."

"Y' know," said Guilliani, "a guy sells arms, he isn't re-sponsible for what other guys do with 'em. I mean, that's a simple fact, right?"

"I'm not interested in your responsibility for what happened," Bolan argued. "That's between you and the NYPD. All I want to know is who bought the Piat."

"You put me in an awkward position," said Guilliani.

"*Dead* is awkward," Bolan responded grimly.

Guilliani glanced up again. "I think I really do know who you are," he said. "Nobody else would have got into my place... So, what the hell? I sold two of the things to some gooks. I did a deal in North Africa some time back, and the guys I did business with wanted to unload these two toys...with a dozen bombs. I took 'em. Figured they might be good for somethin' someday."

"Who bought them?"

Guilliani sighed. "Okay. Gooks. Vietnams, you said. Okay, Vietnams. When I read the story in the paper this morning, I saw how my two bomb launchers had been used. I figured somebody would come calling. So I tried to figure out just who exactly bought those damn things. I do business for cash, you understand, and don't keep much in the way of records."

"Get on with it," grunted Bolan.

"Okay. Well, the best I can figure is, the tubes and bombs were sold to a Viet named Pete Nhu. He's bought some other stuff. The guy has money. Don't ask me where he's from. New York somewhere, of course. He pays cash. No questions asked, either side. And that's the best I can tell ya."

Bolan glanced back toward the station where a firefight had just left three men dead. "Cops ever come?" he asked Guilliani.

Guilliani grinned. "When I call 'em," he said. "Don't worry. I'll clean up your mess. You and I got no beef. Right? You and I got no beef."

Bolan didn't answer. He knew what would come next, but he didn't care. In fact, it was part of his plan. After the intruder had left, Dolfy July wasted no more time. He shouted a few terse orders, then sat down to make a quick telephone call.

"It's in the fan, buddy. I just had a visit from—"

"I don't care who you had a call from, so long as you didn't tell them anything."

"You aren't listenin', Pete. So *listen,* dammit!"

"You didn't talk?"

"What the hell's the difference? You think what you did is a goddamn secret? *Listen to me!* The guy took out Tommy Savvy. Huh? Who takes out a guy like Tommy Savvy? Plus two more guys.

"Got it? One guy. An' he left me a souvenir. A sharp-shooter's medal! You listenin'? I said a sharpshooter's medal."

"And you gave him my name?" Pete Nhu asked coldly.

"I'd have given him my grandmother," said Guilliani. "I'm lucky I got my head on. But . . . hey, Pete! Your name means nothin' to him!"

"It is . . . *my name,* Dolfy," said Nhu coldly. "The man who hands out sharpshooters' medals— It's a start for him. I owe you one, Dolfy."

"Well, don't come and try to play with me the game you played with the spics, Pete," said Guilliani coldly. "I'm not defenseless. I'm not a spic, and I'm not a mustache. Hey, I didn't have to warn you. Don't forget that. I didn't have to call."

The line was dead. Nhu had hung up.

Guilliani glanced around. "Move it!" he yelled. His men were packing the best stuff into trucks. They were moving.

LUISA GOYA KNELT AND WEPT by the caskets of her husband and her two children. The little ones lay in small white caskets, her husband, Carlos, in a big bronze one. They were lying amid fragrant wreaths in a funeral home operated by an immensely fat lay preacher.

The archbishop had ruled that no priest would pray for the souls of her little family. The marriage was not valid in the eyes of the church, and the children were not legitimate. Anyway, she and her husband were criminals, engaged in the trade in illegal substances.

So that was how it was. It hardly counted compared to the mind-numbing grief she felt. She knelt and she prayed, and in the purse by her knees on the floor was the automatic she had fired from the window that tragic night. The priest would never know how close she had come to putting a couple of slugs in his belly when he refused to accept her husband and children for religious burial.

But why kill the priest? Or the archbishop who had turned down her appeal?

Luisa Goya had different quarry in mind. The Vietnamese.

She had what she needed.

Before the cops searched last night, she'd put all the guns in her handbag—and what cop was going to search a young mother who had just lost her husband and two children? She hadn't really examined what Carlos had had in the flat. Three guns. She knew how to use one, and she would figure out how to use the other two.

She had nothing more to lose, and she herself was someone to be reckoned with now. There wasn't a man in New York who was going to say no to Luisa Goya. Even here, where she knelt by her family's caskets and prayed and wept, the men in the back of the room were staring at her body. So it was a weapon, too.

She would have her revenge. They could talk of the code of *la hombría*. Well, let them. There was another code.

4

Pete Nhu expected to inherit honor and power from the previous night's events—first, the death of the honored one, then the butchery of the Colombians on 146th Street. He was the obvious heir to the leadership that had been lost when the barbarians shot the old man. As he looked around at his associates of the Watchful Hawk, he wondered if anyone would challenge him.

Someone would. Because he was young.

He went down to the basement of the building on White Street. Here—and even the old ones didn't know it—was where he and men like Bob Lac made the stuff. The new stuff. Crank, some called it. But it wasn't like what had gone by that name before. It was new. They had given it a name, a French name—*la sottisse*—meaning the foolish stuff that reduced people to sots. On the streets the new addicts were calling it sotty, their English slang for the French word they didn't understand.

The honored one, Vgo Nguyen Minh, had introduced them to it. He had begun life as a Buddhist monk, but became known to the French as *l'Infidèle*—the Unfaithful. He had found a better living in trade than in the austere life of a monk. Trade stood for whatever was in demand, particularly if it was difficult to get and therefore expensive. Trade in opium, in the bodies of young girls—or young boys, for that matter.

The Americans had made him immensely rich. They wanted everything, and they paid top price. But then they were gone, and the other ones came. But no matter. When a man is rich and shrewd and resourceful, he can manipulate anything. He came out of Vietnam and eventually reached the States, bringing with him the eleven-year-old Nhu and the ten-year-old Lac and six others.

The honored one. That was what he had wanted to be called. Well, he had earned honor. Not least just now, a few months ago when he showed his boys how to make sotty.

It was a mixture. Crack and heroin. A perfect combination. Sotty didn't have to be shot into the veins with a needle that might be dirty. It was smoked. What it supplied was the crack high, but the heroin kept the high going longer and then let you down easy. Perfect. And one dose sold on the street for ten dollars, twice the price of a dose of crack.

The Colombians were furious. Their crack market was disappearing. The trendy kids were smoking sotty.

And that was the reason for the recent events, and no doubt that would be the cause of everything that was yet to come down that day and the next.

"SHE'LL TALK," Doctorow said. "She wants to talk."

Bolan had come back across the river from his confrontation with Dolfy July to find that the word was out. You couldn't keep a deal like that secret. The afternoon radio news broadcast were calling the firefight in the abandoned gas station in Jersey City another skirmish in the gang war that had erupted on the streets of Manhattan last night. And in a way it was.

"I just think you ought to see what you're dealing with," Doctorow said.

They had come to one of the ten drug-treatment centers in New York that were all called Phoenix House. Doctorow introduced Bolan as Mike Belasko, and they went back into the center to meet with a young woman named Susan Cardle.

She was maybe twenty-two or -three years old, a slender girl with great dark eyes and long, graceful fingers. She was emaciated, and, as would be apparent after a moment's talk, she was still a little disoriented.

"The narc..." she said quietly to Doctorow. "Again."

"This is Mike Belasko, Susan," said Doctorow. "He's not a narc. But I'd appreciate it if you'd tell him about the stuff you were smoking."

She smiled lazily. "Man..." she began. "If the stuff wouldn't kill you, it would be *great*."

"What is it, Susan?" asked Doctorow. "I know, sure, but tell Mike."

"Well..." she said. "You get a little pipe. I mean, a real little pipe. And you stuff the mixture down in the pipe. And you smoke it. You get your crack, and you get your shit, all in the same smoke. An', man, it's *dreamy*."

"And no needle, huh, Susan?" asked Doctorow.

"No AIDS, man. I got no AIDS."

"What's the downside, Susan?"

She turned down the corners of her mouth. "I'm *addicted*," she muttered. "The shit... I mean, you know, properly called heroin. You get hooked. I'm hooked. Like I wasn't on the other stuff. I mean, I can't live without it. I'm tryin', man, but I don' know how I'm gonna live without it."

"So where'd you buy the stuff?"

"Street," she said. "Where you buy it all. They're...you know, Orientals. Using the stuff is called chasing the dragon. Lots of people chasing the dragon these days."

As Bolan and Doctorow left the center, Doctorow explained, "Heroin. It was out of style, really out. Never was chic, you know. You had to shoot it, and the trendy people didn't like that. But this way...they smoke it. Just when the number of heroin addicts began to fall, this new method appeared."

"'Chasing the dragon,'" said Bolan.

"What the old junkies used was about twelve percent pure," said Doctorow. "What they use in sotty is forty-five percent. A whole new market for heroin. And it's always been the worst thing around. Crack is nothing compared to sotty. A new epidemic."

"A new job," Bolan said. "A new war."

ON A HOT SUMMER DAY, a man wearing a nylon jacket would be conspicuous on the streets of New York. The men in jeans and shorts matched them with light T-shirts or polo shirts. But under an outfit like that, there was no way to conceal the Beretta. Bolan had no choice but to dress like a businessman. He wore a white shirt and tie, with a summer-weight dark blue blazer and khaki slacks. There was room under his arm for the leather cradling the 93-R. He carried a couple of extra clips, one in each jacket pocket.

Those were his hunting clothes for the streets of New York. In late afternoon he went hunting for dealers.

Doctorow had told him that to find the guys who deal in sotty, there was no need to go to the mean streets. In fact, the stuff wasn't used by down-dirty junkies; they couldn't afford it. Bolan would find it in good neighborhoods.

"If I can find it, why can't the cops?"

"They can. But what good does it to do bust a street dealer? He won't say where he gets the stuff, and you can't force him to tell. So pretty soon he's out on bail. Even if he isn't, there are plenty of others to take his place."

"So you and the NYPD can't find your way up the line?"

"We haven't done very well so far."

"I'll make 'em come to me," said Bolan.

He started among the parked cars in what should have been a park but had been made a parking lot by the politicians—in front of city hall.

The trade was not secret at all. Men came down the steps of city hall, walked into the parking lot, slipped past a dealer, passed money, got little envelopes and walked on, stuffing their buys into their pockets. It was that open.

But the Vietnamese dealers in sotty hadn't taken this turf yet. These dealers were Colombians, dealing crack and coke. Their soldiers stood around too, watching for interference.

They had become wary and far less cocky than they had been just a day ago.

But they weren't driven off their turf, and surely they didn't mean to be. Somewhere in town they had to be holding a council of war. The war between them and the Watchful Hawks wasn't over.

Seeing that the Colombians still held the city hall turf, Bolan walked down Broadway, then into the financial district. Wall Street, Exchange Place, Bowling Green. There, among the clustered skyscrapers, past the stock exchange, were some of the richest banks in the world.

This was the territory for sotty. For the urbane young men and women of the brokerage houses and law firms. The stock traders. The wheelers and dealers. They would want the newest thing, and they would pay for it.

The dealing was a little more subtle here. In fact, it would have been difficult to detect except for one thing: the dealers were all Vietnamese.

It was the same routine with a little twist. Rushed young men in their shirtsleeves, crisp, pretty young women in light summer dresses, hurried out onto the sidewalk, made their buys and disappeared back inside.

The soldiers did not stand apart staring. They strolled along the sidewalk, dressed in dark suits, clutching briefcases. Once again, if they had not all been Vietnamese, they might easily have been overlooked. Bolan had no doubt that their dark suits concealed heavy iron, and that they carried the street supply of sotty in those briefcases.

On this block, just one man worked. In the next block, two. They seemed to work in pairs—one dealer, one soldier.

Traffic was brisk. Doctorow had said the going price was ten dollars a pop. If so, the dealer he was watching was making two hundred dollars an hour. Except he was making a lot more than that, because some of his customers were taking three or four pops.

The soldiers moved in and, as Bolan had figured, let the dealer unload from the briefcase into his pockets.

Dealers and soldiers. The way it was going, there had to be a bigger supplier somewhere in the neighborhood.

He kept his eyes open. Yeah. The way he'd figured. Along came a black Mercedes. The soldier stepped off the curb. Somebody in the back seat of the Mercedes handed out a new briefcase and took the one the soldier was carrying. The supply.

So Bolan had three choices. Take the dealer, take the soldier, take the Mercedes.

Why the dealer? Or the soldier? Now that he knew about the Mercedes, why not go for the big game?

He had to wait. Briefcases had just been traded. It might be another hour before this dealer sold what the supplier had just delivered. So, okay. Time to watch the dealing. Time to study the dealer and the soldier. And the customers.

A NYPD car cruised past. The dealer walked along the street as if he were hurrying to keep an appointment. The car passed on into the next block. The dealer turned to go back to where he had been, but before he could reach that spot, first one customer stopped him, then another, and the market had shifted places.

A black man in shabby clothes approached the dealer. He said something, and the dealer shook his head. The soldier moved in. In seconds the soldier was pushing the black man along, hustling him away from the dealer and the stream of customers who might be turned off by the old junkie.

The customers weren't junkies. They were bright young people, alert and clear-eyed. For now. The stuff hadn't got them yet. But it would.

Actually it already had, because they knew what sotty was, knew the danger, but they bought it anyway. They already used cocaine and crack, and all but a few of them were addicted, though probably none of them would admit it.

They were on a slide into hell, and most of them would slide all the way.

Bolan watched the next block for a while, then went back to where the one dealer and one soldier worked.

The Mercedes returned.

The soldier stepped off the curb as before. The car door opened. The soldier and the man in the back seat, intent on exchanging briefcases, didn't see the big man in the crisp-looking blazer. The soldier never did see him, because Bolan's fist, crashing against his ear, stunned him, and he fell to his hands and knees, shaking his head, baffled and struggling to sort out earth and sky. Bolan grabbed the supplier by the hand that held out the briefcase and threw him to the sidewalk.

In two seconds Bolan was in the back seat of the Mercedes. He slammed the door, then drew the Beretta and laid it against the back of the driver's neck.

"Move."

As a wary crowd formed around the staggered soldier, still on his hands and knees on the street, and the supplier, sprawled awkwardly on the sidewalk, the Mercedes sped away.

"It is yours," said the driver. "I will get out, drive away. The car is yours, the money, the stuff. I didn't sign on to die for it."

"Drive up to Central Park," said Bolan. "No funny business, you're not going to die."

The driver turned right and right again, heading for the South Street Viaduct. He glanced at Bolan in the rearview mirror.

"You are," he said. "Going to die, I mean. Hey, man, I don't know you, okay? Never saw you before. You look like a million guys. Like, I couldn't identify you if my life depended on it—which it probably will, if you don't waste me."

"I'm not going to kill you," Bolan repeated.

The driver was not Vietnamese. Maybe he was Italian, maybe Greek...maybe even Turkish. He was all New Yorker.

The back seat of the car was filled with briefcases, two dozen of them. Bolan began opening them. They were stuffed with heat-sealed clear plastic envelopes. Some of the envelopes contained the white powder, cocaine. Most of them contained little brown rocks of sotty. Each envelope sold for ten dollars. Some of the briefcases were crammed with cash.

"There's more in the trunk," the driver said helpfully.

Bolan flipped curiously through the unsorted bills in one of the briefcases. Twenties. Fifties. A few tens. Mostly twenties and some fifties. The customers didn't buy singles.

Okay. Let the animals who dealt in this stuff pay some of the expenses. He pulled off a few hundred dollars in fifties and stuffed them in his jacket pocket. Then— What the hell? Some more in the other pocket of his jacket. Enough to cover some costs. Not more.

When the car was running at speed up the FDR Drive, Bolan began to tear open envelopes and pour the little brown rocks out the window. They fell on the pavement and were ground to dust by the traffic.

"You know what those envelopes are worth each, buddy?"

"I know."

"Then, hell, you aren't— And you aren't a narc, either. So what the hell...?"

"I've got something for you," said Bolan. "You're going to live to talk to your bosses. Give them this. A gift from me. They'll know what it is."

He pressed a sharpshooter's medal into the hand of the driver, who had reached back to get it.

The man looked at it. "Hell, I know what this is," he said in a breaking, guttural voice. "And who that makes you."

"Nice to meet you," Bolan said.

The driver shuddered. "Man... No problems. Okay? I'll deliver the message."

"You got it."

In Central Park the driver cruised until he found a spot north of the reservoir where only a few people were around. He pulled the car to the side, just off the pavement in the grass.

"Now what I want you to do," Bolan said, "is help me pile the briefcases behind the car, and under."

The driver—likely Italian, now that Bolan had a better look at him—was eager to cooperate. He opened the trunk and began to stack attaché cases under the rear.

"I think I know what you got in mind," he said to Bolan. "You know how much—"

"I don't give a damn," said Bolan.

"No. Don't give a damn."

Within two minutes the briefcases from the trunk and those from the back seat were piled around the back of the car, shoved under as far as they would go.

"Got a match?" Bolan asked.

The driver tossed over some wooden matches in a box imprinted with the name of an expensive restaurant. He stood back and watched Bolan with mixed apprehension and fascination.

Bolan knelt and took aim at the gas tank of the Mercedes. The silenced Beretta made hardly a pop and attracted no attention in the park as the 9 mm slug punched through the tank and gasoline began to pour over the briefcases filled with sotty and money.

"More distance you make, the better chance you got to get away from here before the cops come," he said to the driver.

The man gave a high sign with one hand and hurried away. He veered off the road into the grass, toward a grove of trees.

Bolan lit a match and tossed it. The gas exploded, the ruptured tank spewed flame and the drugs and money went up in fire.

Bolan walked away across the park. At first, people looked at him curiously, then no one even noticed him. The ones who had seen him toss the match moved away quickly, then in typical New York style, turned to their own interests—picnics, bicycles, running, walking their dogs, making love.

THE VIEW OF KENNEDY AIRPORT was eerie. Orange lights reflected off the clouds and cast a dim light on the streets, but an upward look revealed the brilliant white lights of the incoming planes from all over the world. Others were taking off, the late-evening traffic for Europe, which would arrive at destinations early in the morning.

People lived around the airport. Some of them got used to the constant stream of roaring jets and some didn't.

Doctorow said they sold here, too. Okay. Doc was a narc. He ought to know.

The residents who lived in the neighborhoods around JFK were not the kind of high rollers Bolan had seen in the financial district. No way. That kind didn't live here. They were owners of pizza parlors, muffler shops, dry cleaners, liquor stores, doughnut shops, appliance stores, gas stations, used-car lots. Small businesses. They lived small, tight lives, always on the line between huge success and disgraceful failure. And that meant that they, too, were interested in marijuana, coke, crack and now sotty.

Not heroin. Not the shoot-in-your-arm kind of heroin. That was for the kind of people they despised. As they saw themselves, they were recreational drug users, people who only wanted some fun to relieve the tedium of long days in marginally rewarding businesses. So there was a market, and where there was a market, there were people ready to supply it.

They were not as open about it as the dealers in the financial district. The dealing was not as frenzied.

In the financial district, everything was frenzied. They traded in stocks the same way they traded in narcotics: fast, with an eye to the future, never an eye looking back. Here people looked at the money they handed over for an envelope of sotty—looked at it before they gave it to the dealer—and expected to receive value for money.

Not only that, but as successive gangs of dealers in various substances had learned, the respectable families of Ozone Park and Howard Beach were entirely capable of sweeping their streets clean of whatever they regarded as undesirable. Sotty sold for ten dollars in the financial district. It sold for six here. Behind the bland facades of little frame houses lived families whose sons would go after the guys who were cheating mom and pop.

Apart from that, the trade was not much different. It was slower, but still profitable enough. The little vial or envelope of sotty that sold for ten dollars in Wall Street and six in Ozone Park, cost the dealer two dollars, the distributor fifty cents and the manufacturer just fourteen cents.

For this probe, Bolan wore jeans and a nylon jacket. The Wall Street outfit would have looked odd in Ozone Park. The Beretta rode comfortably in its rig. The evening was a little too warm for the jacket, but it was not conspicuous. Heat or not, other guys walked these streets in the jackets emblazoned with the names of their industrial-league softball teams.

The dealers understood. A Vietnamese was noticeable on these streets, so they tried to be as much as possible like the other ethnic elements.

The warrior could see them on the streets. Dealers and soldiers, just like downtown, though not on every block. There wasn't enough business. It appeared that most establishments were strapped for business.

Outside a pizza parlor whose neon sign threw garish pink light over half a block, he was hailed by a busty, hippy girl in a bursting halter and tight, skimpy shorts.

"Hey, big fellow. Lonesome?"

"Not really."

She sighed. "Figures," she said. "If you got an amateur at home, I can do better. I do what no amateur even heard of."

"No doubt, honey," Bolan said, "but I've got something else in mind."

"You'd be better off with what I've got in mind," she said.

He grinned at the blond hooker. And noted that her eyes were dark, her complexion olive. Only her hair was bleached an unnatural yellow.

"Tell you what. Twenty bucks for a tip."

"Tip?"

"Who's the dealer?" he asked. "I think I see, but I don't wanna take a chance on walking up to a narc and asking for something."

She laughed. "Narc! You kiddin'? Last time I seen a narc was when one busted *me,* and didn't even have a pop of anything on me. Hey...twenty for a steer? You kiddin'? You're a narc yourself."

He shook his head. "Here's the twenty, like it was for something else. Just point."

"Point my achin' backside," she said. "And get had for a pointer? Hey, I ain't a pointer. A setter maybe. But okay." She took the twenty-dollar bill. "See the little guy in the red jacket? That's him. You want a pop, that's who you see."

"Who's the soldier?" Bolan asked.

"Soldier?"

"If somebody wanted to heist the guy, which one would come out of the woodwork?"

The hooker grinned. "Don't turn your head. He's watchin' us. In the pizza joint. Ol' buddy never moves out of the pink light. The gook in the pizza joint watches.

Lemme have another twenty for that info, buddy. Then you an' me walk way into the dark, like we'd made a deal. The gook misses nothin', and if you're figurin' some hassle with those guys, I don't wanna have them know I told you *anythin'*."

"Deal," Bolan said, and he handed her the second twenty, took her by the arm and led her away along the street and out of the light shed by the pizza parlor.

"Forty bucks..." she said quietly when they were out of sight from the pizza joint. "Thanks, buddy. You damned hunk. I'd give the regular stuff to you *free*."

"Thanks. Another time I'll come back and take you up on that."

She grinned. "Sure you will," she tossed knowingly at him, and she walked off into the night, her backside bouncing provocatively.

Bolan did her a favor. He did not move back toward the pizza parlor too fast. Let the soldier inside think he'd stayed with the girl long enough for him to have used her services. Staying back along the street, in the dark, gave him a chance to watch the dealer at work.

A pattern emerged. Cars pulled up to the curb, and the deals were made without the drivers even stepping out.

A supplier car came along every little while to replenish the dealer's supply and take the money. The supplier/collector came more often out here, but there was no briefcase involved. Business was slower, and the dealer had only what was in his pockets.

Bolan again decided to go for the supplier. Like this afternoon. No point in taking the dealer. The dealers had to get taken from time to time: it was a part of the cost of doing business. But a couple of hits on supplier cars in one day would make the Watchful Hawks sit up and take notice.

The car was a white Saab with two men: the driver, and supplier/collector in the back seat.

The kids in front of the pizza parlor pretended they didn't see it. It wasn't smart to be obvious about watching dealers at work. They turned and looked away. The Vietnamese inside kept his eye on them, then fixed his attention on the car and the dealer.

As the exchange took place—a little slower because the dealer had to empty his pockets into the hands of the man in the rear seat—Bolan trotted out of the shadows.

The man in the pizza parlor saw and rushed to the door.

Bolan threw the dealer aside, sending him sprawling along the curb, and leveled the muzzle of the Beretta on the supplier/collector.

"Out."

Shaking his head but holding his hands out and apart to show he was not drawing a weapon, the Vietnamese came out of the car as Bolan backed up a couple of paces.

The driver jammed the car in gear and gunned the engine. Bolan lowered the 93-R and loosed a 3-round burst into the left rear tire. The tire exploded and dropped the Saab on the wheel rim, but it lurched forward just the same, dragging a fender on the curb.

Bolan had not forgotten the hardman from the pizza parlor, who now stood on the curb opposite, legs apart, taking aim with a snub-nose revolver. He fired. The range was only fifty feet, but even at that range a gunner without long practice is hard put to hit a man with a snub-nose .38. The bullet drilled past.

Bolan drove his left fist into the face of the supplier and dropped him out of the way. He flipped the 93-R into single-shot mode. The gunner was setting himself to try again. Because of the kids on the sidewalk, Bolan aimed for his chest, and the Beretta spit almost silently. The gunner let go of his snub-nose and clutched his chest. He dropped to his knees, then doubled over.

The Saab was still moving, the dragging rear fender tearing and spewing sparks. The car had covered fifty yards or so.

Bolàn flipped down the front handgrip on the Beretta, hooked his thumb through the big trigger guard and thrust the pistol out with both hands. He took time to aim, then loosed one shot.

The shot punched through the rear window of the Saab and traveled on to shatter the windshield. The driver flung open the door, jumped out and ran.

Bolan sprinted forward. All the regular pedestrian traffic had cleared the street, and no other cars were driving through. As he had done with the Mercedes in the afternoon, he put two shots into the gas tank. When the stream of gasoline had run along the street some thirty or forty feet, he tossed a match. Fire spread back along the stream to the tank, and the car exploded. Once again, money and sotty burned in a boiling, smoky fire.

The supplier/collector sat on the pavement, clutching his broken nose. He was alone. The dealer had run.

Bolan walked back to the Vietnamese with the bloody nose. He tossed a sharpshooter's medal on the pavement in front of him.

"Take that to your bosses," he said. "Tell them to add it to their collection. I'll have some more for them."

5

"So. You don't know what this is," said Air Marshal Le Xuan Diem. "I am not surprised. But *I* do."

Bui Dang Nhu took from the marshal's extended hand the small medal he had given him to examine. "But I think I know what it is. A sharpshooter's medal."

"Yes," said Marshal Diem. "Something the Americans earned for honorable achievement with their weapons. But today, in this country, it means something different. A man who earned it uses it as a token. He leaves it where he takes his vengeance, as a sort of signature. You have heard of him? The Executioner.

"He doesn't like the business you are in, Pete. Also, some other lines of business. He has very direct methods of eliminating those businesses—and the people engaged in them. He was a fighter in our country in the old days. You know what a penetration specialist was? You should know. A man to be reckoned with. A very dangerous man, let me warn you."

"Seriously?" asked Pete Nhu.

"Seriously. If this man has elected you for his special attention, you have very big trouble."

"We seem to be fighting two wars," said Pete Nhu. "Against the spics and now against this American."

"Not any American," Marshal Diem corrected. "The Executioner."

"Can the Colombians have hired him?" questioned Nhu.

Marshal Diem shrugged. "He is not for hire. Not by the likes of them, anyway. No, I think you've stirred him up.

When you shot up that apartment building on 146th Street—"

"No," Pete Nhu disagreed firmly. "He could not have become involved so soon. Within hours after—"

The marshal interrupted. "Within hours after you attacked the Colombians, the Executioner paid a call on your arms dealer." He made a dismissive gesture. "Well ... the man had the reputation of being a phantom, a ghost. Maybe he is."

"In one day," said Nhu, "he went to my arms supplier and drove him out of business. That's what happened. Dolfy July moved out of Jersey City. The sharpshooter then attacked two of our supply cars and burned up a million and a half dollars in cash and stuff."

"Street value, the stuff," remarked the marshal blandly.

Pete Nhu nodded. "Street value."

"So. What are you doing about it?" asked Marshal Diem.

Though Pete Nhu had made no firm plans, the one thing he definitely wished to get out of was discussing it with Marshal Diem. The marshal had been no friend of Vgo Nguyen Minh, the honored one. In the old days, back in Saigon, Minh had been arrested several times on his orders, once on suspicion that Minh had tried to arrange his assassination. It was true—the honored one had tried to rid Vietnam of the curse of Diem.

The honored one had entered America illegally and could have been deported. Pete Nhu and Bob Lac were in the same position. But Marshal Diem had arrived as an honored guest of the government of the United States. A hero. Marshal of the Vietnamese air force, unwavering enemy of the Communists. A romantic figure, he had flown out of Saigon only at the last moment, as the Vietcong rampaged through the city.

A token of his old image walked into his office now—a tall striking Vietnamese girl, maybe nineteen years old, dressed in the same style of skintight soft black leather jacket and pants that the late Madame Diem had affected. The marshal himself sat behind his desk in the black leather jacket he had worn as a flyer. The big window air-conditioners labored to keep the marshal's offices and quarters cool enough to let him and the girl wear leather in midsummer. But it was an element of his image and something he would not surrender.

Nor would he surrender cigars and aviator's sunglasses.

Marshal Diem kept an office on East Forty-third Street, near the United Nations, where he was supposed to represent a South Vietnamese government-in-exile. In truth, he was not accredited to the UN and could not even enter the buildings except as a tourist. How he earned his living was a mystery.

It was no mystery to Pete. He knew.

"I can perhaps relieve you of the burden of the Executioner," Marshal Diem offered.

"You can relieve me of a ghost, of a phantom?" Pete Nhu asked, not without a touch of irony in his voice.

"I have the means," the marshal said with quiet confidence.

"Your price?"

"One million dollars cash. Let us say twenty thousand fifty-dollar bills. Ten percent down, when we shake hands on the agreement, ten percent more tomorrow when I will have made my arrangements and will need to put some money around, and eighty percent when the fabled Executioner is dead."

Pete Nhu extended his hand. "Your down payment will be delivered within the hour," he said.

"SOMEONE IS DOING IT for us," said Juan Llorente. "Two of their cars yesterday—"

"*Two!*" yelled Francisco Pardo. "One dead. Maybe a million dollars. Maybe two. What is that compared to what we lost? Are we to stand around and wait for some mysterious stranger to avenge—"

"Just who is the 'mysterious stranger,' Francisco?" asked Llorente. "Surely we can't rely on strangers. Who is he? The Lone Ranger? Batman?"

"We don't know yet," Pardo admitted sullenly.

Juan Llorente was not a member of the Colombian Council of Señors, but he was only one step below. He was a man whose word had to be heeded. Fifty years old, he was a veteran of many wars. Bald, with dark liver spots on his scalp, he was loose and heavy and believed he was entitled to be comfortable.

"Find out who he is," Llorente instructed. "He may be more dangerous to us than the gooks. We may have to take him out. Find out, Francisco. And don't take too much time doing it."

OFFICIALLY Captain Francis O'Brien had no idea who Doc Doctorow's friend was. Had he known, he would have been obliged to arrest him. Unofficially, as a shrewd old cop, he had a pretty good idea who the man introduced as Belasko really was. He wouldn't tell his subordinates. Certainly he wouldn't tell his superiors. And officially he had to keep his distance from "Belasko" and from what he might do.

"I don't know you," he said with a sly grin. "Never saw you. If you're the guy that hit the dealers in the financial district and Ozone Park, I don't know it."

"It's your town," Bolan said. "What next?"

The captain glanced at Doc Doctorow. "Well," he began, "several months ago the Viets took over the neighborhood above the United Nations. You know, places like the streets around Tudor City, where a lot of UN diplomats live. Lots of expensive apartments around there. Those UN people think they're damned sophisticated, so they go for the new junk—whatever's the newest thing."

Doctorow took up the story. "The Colombians resent the loss of that turf. There've been some battles on the streets, but so far the Vietnamese have managed to hang on to it. We've been expecting trouble there."

"I think I'll go have a look," said Bolan.

"And maybe I'll go with you this time," Doctorow added. "Unofficially, of course."

Bolan didn't protest, so the two of them headed for Tudor City, a small enclave of handsome old brick apartment buildings, a community apart, on the high ground above First Avenue and the United Nations.

On such a bright Saturday afternoon, people walked their dogs on the streets and on the shady lawns of Tudor City. Au pairs—French and English girls brought to the States to work a year or two as live-in baby-sitters for prosperous families—wheeled infants in baby carriages and led toddlers in little harnesses, taking the children out for the air and sun. Men and women jogged on the sidewalks, dressed in white, equipped with fancy running shoes and listening to their personal tape players as they huffed and sweated along the streets.

Bolan strolled along, the Beretta in its usual spot under his light blue sport coat.

In a short while he confirmed that the operation was in place. The dealer was a small, modest-looking man, wearing a blue blazer with gold buttons, gray slacks, a white shirt and striped tie. With his silver-rimmed eyeglasses he looked like a staff member from a UN mission. He sat on a park bench with an attaché case on his lap, reading the *New York Times*.

He did his business inconspicuously. People stepped up to him, spoke quietly as if they were asking directions or commenting on the weather, and the deal was made discreetly, the envelope and money being exchanged under the newspaper.

"I can tell you his name," said Doctorow. "Phan Duc Cao. The young ones call him Brown Cao, and he doesn't like it. He was a colonel in the Vietnamese army. He's got a certain prestige in the Viet community in New York."

"I know him," Bolan said.

"From Vietnam?"

Bolan nodded. "Battle of Dak To. He was a good officer, a brave soldier."

"Well, he—"

"I'm going to speak to him. Why don't you wait for me? You don't want to know him."

Bolan walked across the street. As he approached the bench where Cao sat, other Vietnamese appeared—the older man's protection. They kept a distance, but they were wary and ready to move.

Bolan sat down beside the distinguished-looking man. "Hello, Colonel Cao," he said. "Do you remember me?"

Cao looked up, his eyes filled with alarm. Then he frowned, his mouth fell open and he nodded. "Ah...I might have suspected you were in New York, Sergeant Bolan. It has been a very long time."

He extended his hand, and Bolan shook it. The protection dropped back out of sight.

"I'm surprised to find you in this business," said Bolan.

Cao shrugged. "I was driven from my country. You may call me a refugee. I must earn a living."

"Not this way."

"What else? I have no profession."

Bolan nodded at the briefcase. "That stuff is deadly."

"If we did not supply this market, others would. In fact, others are very anxious to supply it."

"You make yourself my enemy, Colonel."

"I regret that, Sergeant Bolan."

Bolan glanced around. At least three young Vietnamese were keeping an eye on the colonel and the stranger. Colonel Cao probably felt secure.

It was unlikely that the colonel's bodyguards were ordinary thugs, just as it was unlikely that he was pressed to make a living. It was difficult to think that Phan Duc Cao was poor or that he was served by lesser men than had served him in Vietnam.

"Colonel—"

A motorcycle raced around the corner from Forty-first Street, its unmuffled engine roaring. Instinctively Bolan threw his body across the colonel's—though he was under no obligation to protect the man—and grabbed the Beretta from under his jacket.

Two people rode on the motorcycle—a man and woman from the look of them—the man gripping the handlebars and throttle and accelerating as he sped toward the bench, the woman leveling the muzzle of an automatic weapon.

She got off only the initial rounds of a burst before the motorcycle hit the curb, hurtled into the air and threw her headlong onto her face on the sidewalk. A Viet guard had gut-shot the driver, who stopped skidding on the sidewalk just in time for the bike to land on top of him.

The screams of women and children filled the air. Those who did not throw themselves on the ground ran as fast as they could.

The woman rose on her hands and knees and crawled toward the Uzi that had flown from her hands. A slug drilled through her, toppling her to the grass at the edge of the sidewalk.

But the attack was far from being over. Two more motorcycles skidded into Tudor City Place. The gunner on the lead bike sprayed the east side of the street with slugs, getting one of Cao's protectors. The fire ripped through the glass of a restaurant, propelling a torrent of glass over the tables inside.

The second bike came on, the gunner leaning out to fire on the little tableau of Colonel Cao and the man covering him.

Bolan took out the biker with a 9 mm slug through the throat, and the bike spun around and threw the gunner to the street. The spinning rear wheel of the bike caught the gunner's foot in its spokes and then mangled his leg as he screamed in agony.

A Vietnamese stepped from between two buildings and calmly shot the screaming man.

Suddenly a dark blue Ford careened around the corner. Only Bolan, who was on the west side of the street, saw what was coming down. There was no Uzi to contend with here. A man in the back seat wrenched the pin from a grenade.

Bolan fired before there was time to toss the grenade. Struck in the face, the attacker fell back, and the grenade rolled from his hands to the floor of the car. The driver jerked the parking-brake handle, flung open the door and threw himself out of the car while it skidded and fishtailed. He hit the street hard and rolled, arms and legs flopping and bones breaking.

The grenade went off inside the car.

A Vietnamese walked over to the driver where he lay groaning on the street and shot him in the head.

The Ford caught fire and began to burn. The street had become almost quiet. Two motorcycles lay on their sides. Five Colombians were sprawled dead on the street, as was one Vietnamese. The body of another Colombian burned in the car.

People staggered to their feet, stunned. Children, who had fallen silent in terror, began to cry again.

"I think neither of us wish to be here when the police arrive," Colonel Cao said calmly.

"No," Bolan admitted.

"I am in your debt," said the colonel.

"I was in yours," Bolan replied. "Now we're even."

The colonel brushed down his clothes and picked up his briefcase. "Even," he repeated. "Very well."

"And on opposite sides," Bolan added as a reminder of where he stood.

"I regret it. It need not be."

"Yes, it does," said Bolan. "It has to be."

Colonel Phan Duc Cao nodded. "Then goodbye, my former friend," he said. "I hope we do not meet again."

"THERE'S GOT BE AN END, dammit!"

Captain Francis O'Brien had got the goods from Bolan and Doctorow on the shooting at Tudor City Place. They had met at a hot-dog cart on the street and casually moved away with cans of soft drinks.

O'Brien, in civilian clothes, looked even more red-faced than usual. "Nothing like this has ever happened before. I mean, we had the Five Families wars, some of them pretty bad, and we've had mass shooting among the Colombians. But this—"

"You've got the new Chinese gangs," Doctorow interrupted.

"But they kill each other one or two at a time," the captain retorted. "Can you imagine the heat I'm getting?"

"We're lucky in one thing," Bolan said. "No innocent people were hit."

"That's thanks to you," Doctorow remarked. "You took out some of those shooters before they could spray the whole neighborhood with slugs."

"We had a couple of people injured by flying glass in that restaurant," said Captain O'Brien. "Not seriously, fortunately."

"The Colombians will strike again," warned Doctorow. "They didn't get Colonel Cao, so they'll hit somewhere else. They're behind in this war, and they don't like it."

O'Brien summed it up. "Sooner or later civilians are going to get hurt."

"We don't have much time," Bolan said.

"Right," O'Brien agreed. "We got no time at all."

As IT WAS, the Executioner was the only one who could move fast.

O'Brien was a capable officer, but the NYPD was an immense muscle-bound bureaucracy that locked him inside a tangle of rules. What was more, he was attacked on all sides by people who were sure the police were more dangerous than the criminals and obstructed his every effort to sweep the drug dealers off the streets.

Bill Doctorow was a competent narc, but he too was frustrated by organization and regulation.

It was the old story. Mack Bolan had heard it for more years than he could remember. If only a brave and honest man could—

Sure. Well, *he* could. Without sanction and outside the rules, he worked his own way and took his risks. And guys who admired him couldn't acknowledge him.

LUISA GOYA WAS SUSTAINED by sheer hate.

She had all her husband's guns—the little automatic he had carried when he was dealing, a bigger automatic and a revolver. She didn't understand very well how the automatics worked, and she found the big one difficult to cock. The revolver impressed her as simpler and more reliable. Besides, she had found a full box of ammunition for it. It was in her handbag now, as she walked along Forty-second Street, nudging her way through the crowd.

She had read the words stamped into the stainless-steel frame of the revolver. It was made by Sturm, Ruger and was called a Redhawk. The stylized bird appeared in a medallion on the wooden grips. She didn't know the caliber of the ammunition, but judged the heavy, flat-nosed bullets were enough to kill the men she was going after. She didn't know they were .41 Magnum slugs. She suspected but didn't know that the three cartridges missing from the box of ammunition had killed two Venezuelans who had tried to steal Colombian turf.

Walking in the bright Saturday-afternoon sunlight on Forty-second Street, Luisa knew she didn't look like a determined woman out to kill, or like a woman who had lost a husband and two children only two nights before. She meant to take advantage of looking like a pretty, carefree hooker. Her breasts moved tautly inside a red T-shirt, her backside swayed enticingly in tight white shorts and the toned muscles of her legs were displayed to best advantage by white high-heeled shoes. Her dark hair hung halfway down her back. She could not hide the deep sadness in her great, dark eyes; but few who saw her would be focusing on her eyes.

For many years Bryant Park, a tiny, tree-shaded park behind the New York Public Library, had been free ground for the trade. Marijuana had been peddled there for forty years, hard drugs for thirty. The Colombians had tried to seize the park for turf, but the police had interfered. The park was truce ground. Anyone could sell anything there.

It was odd. West Forty-second Street was a strip, lined with once-grand movie theaters that now featured mostly sex shows. Prostitutes, male and female, hustled on the sidewalks twenty-four hours a day. Every other kind of hustle was worked there. Scores of cops patrolled in pairs. There was maybe more concentration of police power on West Forty-second Street than on any other six or eight blocks in the city. And on the edge of all this stood the New York Public Library with its peaceful little park for people to sit on benches and read books.

Luisa walked up a couple of steps, through the low wall, and entered the park.

She had never been there before, though she'd heard of it. People did sit and read. Pigeons strutted around, their heads bobbing as they picked up bits of popcorn, an occasional nut or chip.

"Grass? Real Tijuana. The best."

She shook her head at the boy selling marijuana. She looked around and also spotted the crack dealer.

Then she saw her mark. Sotty. The little Vietnamese. In a black suit, even on this summer day, he sat on a bench with an attaché case lying beside him. His supply and his money. The way they always did it.

Luisa walked behind him. In an unpracticed but quick and deadly motion, she drew the Ruger from her handbag and fired one .41 Magnum bullet through the body of Dr. Li Yung Soong, professor of Chinese Language and Culture at Colombia University.

Ch'en Ying-chin, a student of Dr. Li, jumped from a bench and ran toward him. Luisa took him for the usual soldier guarding a dealer, and she fired on him. The bullet struck him in the left shoulder and all but tore off his arm.

A precinct blue-and-white of NYPD shrieked to a halt. Officer Tony Lancione jumped from the car and ran across the sidewalk toward the park, drawing his service revolver. His partner stayed at the wheel and called in the signal.

Luisa saw that the running man was a policeman. Terrified of being shot, of being arrested, she leveled the muzzle of the Ruger and fired on Officer Lancione. Her slug exploded his upper chest, and he fell, dead before he hit the ground.

Luisa ran out of the park on Fortieth Street and continued across Sixth Avenue in a breathless race. No one from the park followed. She walked the one block to the Times Square subway station and hurried down into the complex of gates and platforms. She caught the first train that came in, which happened to be on the BMT Line. She rode only two stops, but when she climbed to the street again, she was far from Forty-second Street and far from the initial police search.

AIR MARSHAL LE XUAN DIEM touched the flame of his lighter to a long, thin cigar. He snapped his fingers at his leather-clad mistress, and she rose from the dinner table and switched off the television set.

They had been watching the evening news, three of them—Marshal Diem, the girl and a third Vietnamese, named Quant Chanh Thang.

Thang, formerly a major and commander of a South Vietnamese ranger battalion, had been tagged by a South Carolina sergeant with the name "Major Thing." The Americans found that hugely funny—and he had been known as Major Thing ever since.

Major Thang walked with a cane and a limp. He had lost part of his right leg in 1967 to flying shrapnel from a mortar shell. He bore also a visible depression in his skull above his left eye, the result of being viciously chopped across the forehead with a heavy revolver. That had been done to him by the Cong political officer who took him in custody after the fall of Saigon in 1975.

He'd escaped from prison a few days later, made his way to the coast and by the force of his personality took command of a small wooden boat that refugees had repaired and were about to launch. After fifteen days at sea, during which one-third of the people in the boat died, they were sighted by an American submarine.

Major Thang enjoyed the same status in the States as Marshal Diem; he was a hero and an honored guest. In spite of the ugly dent in his forehead, he was a handsome man. His face was long, his nose thin, his chin long and sharp and his hair a distinguished-looking gray.

"The Chinese professor is not our problem," Marshal Diem said. He was referring to the news story on the death of Dr. Soong. "In one sense, that is. But in another sense, he is. An Asiatic is not safe on the streets of the city this weekend. The spics have run wild."

Major Thang tossed his head. "Well they might," he said.

"I am concerned about another problem," Marshal Diem said. He reached into his pocket and pulled out a sharp-shooter's medal. "You know what this is?"

The major glanced at it and nodded.

"Bolan," said the marshal.

"*Him?* After all these years?"

"He has been active. Our old ally is a different man now. Or maybe the better way to say it, *we* are different men. Either way, he is a dangerous threat."

Major Thang had a concentrated look on his face. "The last I heard of Sergeant Bolan, he was a fugitive from what the Americans call justice. They wanted to kill him. His country betrayed him just as it betrayed us. The Americans turned coward and pulled out and left us to face the Ho Chi Minh gang alone. And they turned against him, their bra-

vest soldier. Our enemies are his enemies. His enemies are
our enemies."

"Well...maybe," said Marshal Diem. "That is a brave
speech, but I am not sure how it stands now, as between
Bolan and his country. In any case, yesterday he allied himself with the spics, killed some valuable men and robbed our
friends of as much as two million dollars."

"Bolan?"

"Bolan," Marshal Diem affirmed. "Whatever went before, this man is now our dangerous enemy. Major
Thing—"

Major Quant Chanh Thang frowned hard. He did not like
being called "Thing." He wasn't exactly sure what the
Americans meant by the word, but it was a joke and nothing complimentary, that was for sure.

"I want you to kill him."

Major Thang's eyes popped wide. "Me? Why me?"

"If you can find him, you can talk to him...about the old
days. You knew him. He would talk to you. And you can
kill him. Or you can set him up for us to do it. Either way,
I can pay you a good price for the head of Sergeant Mack
Bolan. A good price. Let us say half a million dollars—in
American cash."

"I owe none of these Americans anything."

"Except maybe death," said Marshal Diem.

"Maybe," Major Thang agreed.

6

"There's nothing to choose between them," Doctorow objected. "The Colombians and the Vietnamese."

"Yes, there is," Bolan argued. "What you yourself have called the new viciousness. I never thought I'd see the day when I'd wonder if we weren't better off with Cosa Nostra."

"I can answer that one."

"Anyway, I think I had better pay a visit to our Colombian friends," Bolan said. "I wouldn't want them to think—and I sure wouldn't want the Vietnamese to think—I'm taking sides."

"I can show you where some of them hang out," Doctorow offered hopefully.

"You can *tell* me where some of them hang out," Bolan told him.

AS THE VIETNAMESE HAD their own places like Papillon, so did the Colombians. One of those, situated in Queens, was called Casino Bolivar.

This Saturday night Casino Bolivar was heavily guarded. Every Colombian in the city, whether involved in the trade or not, was apprehensive—fearful of attack by a Vietnamese gang. In fact, on this Saturday night only a few customers sat at the bar or in the booths in the club. They were of two kinds—the dull witted, who did not know the danger, plus the macho swaggerers who thought they were demonstrating bravado by their sheer presence on such a dangerous night.

Bolan had let Doctorow drive him past the establishment before sunset—a soft probe. Now he was back for a hard probe, and more. He was back to let them know that the man who left sharpshooters' medals behind was not just the enemy of the Vietnamese; he was the enemy of all animals who made addicts of children.

He was lucky, maybe. Blue lightning was flashing over the city, and rain had fallen off and on all evening, sometimes hard. So the black windbreaker that hid his iron wasn't out of place. The Desert Eagle hung in its leather, while the Beretta rode smoothly on his hip.

The Executioner had not come for an execution. He didn't know—not for sure, anyway—if anyone here was a killer. He had come to find out and to make himself known.

To guys who didn't want to know him.

Casino Bolivar could have been Archie Bunker's place. Situated between a shoe store and an auto-parts store, at one time it had been a friendly neighborhood bar perched welcomingly on a corner. People had come by in the evenings for a beer or three, to watch a game on the big TV set on the wall behind the bar, to talk or to pick up the girls who were willing.

Then it became closed to the neighborhood. The local bar became a private club where English wasn't spoken and where the patrons didn't want to see guys who did.

It was accepted because people knew that there were bars where they didn't want to see guys who spoke Spanish.

But this was different. Casino Bolivar was a tough hangout for tough guys.

They didn't use what they sold. Not in the club. In fact the guys who sold the stuff were, for the most part, too smart to use it. They knew what it did.

Crack was for other people. Anglos. Blacks. Whoever was fool enough to use it.

Bolan stood in the entryway. Double doors. Stained-glass windows, but nothing fancy. No pictures, just an abstract color design. Two steps up from the sidewalk. Three guys hanging out around the door.

Bolan casually walked up. He tried the door and found it locked. He knocked.

"You want somethin'?" one of the guys asked in heavily accented English.

"Want a beer," said Bolan. "How come the door's locked?"

"Private," replied the man. "Private club. For the members. Nobody else."

He had knocked on the door, so it opened just a crack. A dark, scarred face appeared in the crack. A round-faced man stared curiously at Bolan for a moment, judged him to be Anglo and said, "What do you want?"

Bolan glanced at the three loafers. They were watching and listening.

"A friend of mine asked me to meet him here."

"What friend. What's his name?"

Doctorow had supplied a name and had cautioned that using it would be risky.

"Señor Llorente," said Bolan. "Juan Llorente. Is he here?"

The man opened the door. "No. Not tonight, I don't think. And who are you?"

"Phoenix is the name. Señor Llorente said he would be here. Maybe I'm early."

"What business you have with him?"

Bolan scowled down into the scarred face of the man. "Does the *señor* discuss his business with you?"

The man stepped back from the door. "You come in," he said. "I'll call Señor Llorente."

Bolan glanced back at the three glowering men outside the door, then followed his guide inside the club.

Just inside the doors, Bolan stopped and looked round, making his judgment, identifying the ways out. Men and women looked up at this tall, dark, vaguely threatening Anglo. He stared back. He judged that not a single man—and hardly any of the women—was unarmed.

"While I call, you have a drink. Guest of the club."

Bolan stepped to the bar and ordered a beer.

"*¡Policía!*" gasped a woman sitting at one of the tables. She'd turned her face away from the big Anglo at the bar.

"Luisa," the man with her cautioned, speaking in a low voice. He spoke Spanish. "Luisa, not every strange man you see is a policeman. You weren't identified. That's all that counts."

"They saw me," she said fearfully. "They will remember. They will never forget!"

"And if one of them saw you now?" he asked. He shrugged. "I myself wouldn't know if I saw you on the street."

He was her brother-in-law, brother of her husband, who had been killed in the attack on the building on 146th Street two nights before. Luisa had called him as soon as she got off the subway. José was a businessman. He would know what to do.

The first thing he had done was take her to a beauty salon, where in the back room a big, rough woman had all but shaved her head, had cut her long, dark hair down to within two inches of her scalp. Then she had applied something that stung Luisa's skin and stripped every bit of color out of what little bristle remained. After that, as Luisa sat weeping, the woman had applied a dye that turned the brush-cut hair red. Then the big woman—who seemed to take special pleasure in turning a pretty girl into a grotesque creature—had smeared the skin around her eyes with greenish makeup and had applied a dark brown lipstick.

Carlos would have killed her for turning herself into this spectacle.

She couldn't go to his funeral or her children's funeral. And why? By now she had learned that she had killed a Chinese professor and a policeman. No gooks.

José said he would send her home as soon as he could arrange a fake passport for her. The widow of Carlos Goya would be a suspect in the shooting in Bryant Park. Automatically. That was why she could not go to the funerals tomorrow. Also, when she didn't appear, then she would be a suspect for sure.

So who was the Anglo? He was not here for no reason. He sipped very sparingly of his beer, and his eyes circled the room, making his judgment of everybody and everything. Dressed in black, José said he wasn't a policeman, but Luisa wasn't so sure.

"SEÑOR PHOENIX... Señor Llorente says to tell you he will join you here in a few minutes. In the meanwhile, you are a guest of the club. Is there anything...?"

Bolan shook his head. "Just the beer," he said.

The doorman didn't know he'd let Bolan see the flicker of expression he did not want the big American to see. Bolan could guess what conversation had passed between Llorente and the enforcer at his Queens club. Something to the effect that he wasn't to be allowed to get away, and to use any ploy to keep him there. Most especially, nobody was to try to move against him.

And now Llorente was on his way with his big guns, the gunners he trusted to face a man like Phoenix. Oh, sure. He'd heard of Colonel Phoenix. Everybody deep in this business had heard the name, though nobody wanted to. Then, when they did, ambition took over, and they wanted to meet Colonel Phoenix to see if they could best him.

A lot them had tried. Bolan would just as soon not think of how many had tried.

THE MAN WHO'D ESCORTED Bolan inside tried to be inconspicuous in making his way to the table where José Goya sat with a woman who was most likely his sister-in-law. The word was around that Luisa Goya might have been the shooter in Bryant Park.

He leaned over Goya. "Phoenix," he whispered.

José Goya glanced quickly at the Anglo. He'd noticed him before, but this was— Well, it was inconceivable that the damned Colonel Phoenix could be here. He couldn't just walk in a place like this and stand casually at the bar.

Or could he? The word about Phoenix was that he was just damned fool enough to do a thing like that.

The word was, too, that he got away with it.

The man spoke urgently in Goya's ear. "The girl, she's your sister-in-law? Doesn't make any difference. Put her on him. Distract him. Get him to drink more."

Goya shook his head, annoyed.

"Llorente says so. Llorente says *do* it."

Goya glanced at Luisa. If any young woman could distract a man, she could. He looked at her long, shapely legs, her full bosom. The girl was a *woman*.

He leaned closer to her. "Luisa . . . The Anglo at the bar. Not a cop but maybe worse. Men are coming to take him out. You're the decoy. So get his attention, and keep him busy looking at you."

She shook her head. "No. I—"

José felt like slapping her face, but that would have attracted attention. "You say no?" he whispered furiously. "To *me?* To *us?* Your Carlos never said no. Never. And—" he seized her wrist and squeezed hard "—if I tell you to offer yourself to him, you'll do it! You're the most-wanted criminal in New York tonight. You want to go home? Just do as I tell you."

BOLAN WAS NOT SURPRISED. He'd expected an approach like this. She was bold, but she was surprisingly nervous.

"You all alone, big fellow?" she asked in her sultry voice.

"What I am is a very busy fellow," he said.

"My name is Rosa. You buy me a drink?"

"My money seems to be no good here," he said.

She snapped her fingers at the bartender. "Whiskey and water," she said. "Also, for the *señor* . . . ?"

"I'm doing fine with the beer."

"Two whiskey anyway," she said to the bartender.

The whole scene was off. The woman wasn't what she was pretending to be. Also, the people at the bar and around the room were watching her closely.

These guys were anything but sly. He could see them slipping their hands inside their jackets. Checking their iron, that meant they had to be nervous. A man who was confident of himself and his weapon wouldn't have to check.

And when the woman next to him had put her handbag on the bar, he'd heard a distinct thump. Something heavy in that bag. He could guess what.

"That beer no good," she said. "Try the whiskey. Good whiskey. How you say? *Escocés.*"

"Scotch."

"Yes. Very good."

Though he had watched the bartender pour it, Bolan was not satisfied the Scotch was Scotch—and not Scotch with a few drops of something else in it.

"Only drink beer," he said. "Thanks anyway."

She shrugged. "What you do for fun, big Yankee?"

"Play softball," he said with a little grin.

"Beisbol," she mocked. "Hah! You crazy, you know that?"

She was oddly strained. She smiled, even tried to laugh, but her eyes seemed unable to follow suit. They were filled with sadness. Filled with fear.

Yeah. Fear. She knew what was coming down. Any minute now, the Executioner thought.

Then the double doors opened, revealing a little group. Gunmen if he'd ever seen any.

The girl who called herself Rosa gave a little shriek and jumped away from him.

The first gunner, an immense guy with a black beard and long hair tied at the back of his neck, whipped out an automatic. It looked like a Colt .45. He adopted a spread-out stance and shoved the automatic forward with both hands.

But he took too much time fixing his stance and getting his grip tight.

The blast from the Desert Eagle shook the club room. The muzzle-flash lit the place like yellow-blue lightning. And the .44 Magnum slug heaved the big man off his feet backward into the other gunmen.

The bartender was coming up with a sawed-off shotgun. Bolan swung the Desert Eagle in a wide sweep and crushed the man's nose and cheekbones with the weight. The bartender staggered back into the shelves of bottles behind the bar, leaving the shotgun on the bar.

Two other gunmen shook free from the fallen gunner and drew iron. Bolan laid the Eagle on the bar and grabbed up the sawed-off. As they took aim on him, he let loose both barrels. The gunners fell back through the doors.

Rosa had fumbled in her handbag and come out with a big, deadly-looking revolver. Bolan flung the shotgun at her. It hit her across the nose, and she dropped the revolver as she grabbed at her bleeding nose and crawled away.

Bolan became aware of a man at a table. Bolan had noticed him sitting with Rosa before she came to the bar. But now the man had fumbled a little automatic out from under his jacket, stood up and fired. He missed Bolan. His shot winged the bartender in the left arm.

The man at the table was adjusting his aim, but never got around to firing. A slug from the Eagle blew away the entire right side of his head.

Maybe ten more guns were out. But one by one, slowly, they were lowered to the tables, one or two dropped to the floor. Men held their arms out, hands apart. Women did the same.

Bolan guessed there was at least one car on the street outside, at least one Uzi ready to splatter the doorway with 9 mm. He backed toward the rear door of Casino Bolivar. Just at the end of the bar he paused a moment, reached into a pocket with his left hand and dropped a sharpshooter's medal on the bar.

He hurried through the kitchen. Whoever had been there had left. He switched off the lights before he opened the back door and slipped out into the alley behind the club.

Trotting along the gravel-paved alley, he came around the end of the club building and worked his way along the edge of the building toward the front until he could see the street.

Yeah. Just as he'd figured. A black Cadillac limo. Dark glass windows, so you couldn't see who was inside. But the rear door was open, and standing outside that door was what he'd expected to see—a solid, black-clad man with an Uzi machine pistol ready to fire when somebody came out.

A man ran through the doors of the bar. The muzzle of the Uzi came up, and the man yelled just in time. The man stood between the door and the gunner, telling what had happened in quick, nervous Spanish.

Someone inside the Cadillac spoke. The door opened on the passenger side of the front seat, and another gunman climbed out. He, too, was armed with an Uzi, and he came around the car. The man from inside Casino Bolivar kept talking, and the two gunmen began to look around. Then each of them took a side of the building, and they moved cautiously toward the corners.

One of them, the one who had been standing outside the car, walked toward Bolan.

The warrior decided the time had come to change weapons, to meet this challenge a little differently. He shoved the Desert Eagle back inside its leather and pulled the Beretta.

Bolan backed away, into the shadows between the club and the shoe shop next door. The gunner with the Uzi paused for a long moment on the sidewalk, peering into the shadows. Then he moved in, holding the Uzi out in front of him, finger ready on the trigger.

Bolan dropped to a crouch. He raised the Beretta and took practiced aim on the silhouette slowly moving toward him. The flash hider hid the flash. The sound suppressor contained the crack of the cartridge, and the subsonic bullet flew silently from the muzzle to the forehead of the gunner.

Silence. No one in the club, no one in the street, had the slightest notion a hardman had fallen in the shadows between Casino Bolivar and the shoe store.

The other gunman prowled behind. Bolan turned and was ready for him. He took only a minute to arrive and cautiously called out, "Emilio!"

It was all but too easy. These men had terrorized the streets of New York for so long that they could not imagine any real threat to their swaggering power could possibly appear. Hadn't they made it plain that whoever opposed them would be lucky to die? He would even be lucky if he alone died, and not also his wife and children, anyone related to him, anyone known to be his friend... Who dared oppose such an enemy?

The Executioner dared. His second subsonic round cut through the throat of another Uzi-toting killer.

The man fell, and still the night was silent.

Bolan circled the building and returned to the front of Casino Bolivar on the side of the auto-parts store.

A few men had ventured out. They clustered just outside the double doors, staring at the bodies of the gunmen who had been cut down in the doorway.

The driver was out of the Cadillac now. He stood looking around, staring at the darkness between the club and the adjoining buildings, searching obviously for the two Uzi toters.

Bolan decided to make their understanding complete.

He aimed the Desert Eagle at the idling engine of the Cadillac—idling to keep the air conditioning running and the important man in the back seat perfectly comfortable. Bolan fired. The flare from the muzzle flashed out across the street. The .44 Magnum slug punched through the sheet steel of the hood and slammed into the engine block. The engine stopped. The air conditioning stopped.

Men threw themselves on the ground. No one stood up to contest the warrior.

JUAN LLORENTE STAYED on the floor of the rear seat of his Cadillac until he began to hear sirens. Then he got up and looked around.

People still lay on the ground, on the sidewalk, in the gutter. A few of them—his gunmen—were dead. The rest of them were only terrified.

A young woman, handsome in tight shorts, showing shapely legs, staggered out of Casino Bolivar, clutching her bleeding nose. Odd looking. Close-cropped red hair. Green eye shadow. Still, he thought he recognized her.

"Señor Llorente," she muttered.

"Luisa...?"

"Once Luisa," she mumbled. "Now a widow. Carlos... my little ones... Now José, too."

"José?"

"Dead. Killed by... by that wild man." She began to sob. "What happens to me now, Señor Llorente? I want to go home!"

Llorente glanced around, in the direction of the approaching sirens. "But not a jail cell, ha, Luisa? So come with me. And hurry. This place is about to become dangerous."

TWO HOURS LATER Luisa Goya sat in hot, soapy water in a tub the size of a small swimming pool, in an apartment high above midtown Manhattan. Juan Llorente sat facing her.

"They say you tried to kill him," he said.

Luisa had drunk much champagne. She nodded dully.

"He is a bad man."

She tried to say something in agreement, but her lips were starting to feel numb.

"Maybe he killed Carlos. And your children."

Luisa shook her head. "Gooks," she said.

"But the gooks and this man work together," Llorente insisted. "For many years. The story is that he worked with them in Vietnam."

"He must die," she said woodenly.

FRANCISCO PARDO WAS CONVINCED as well that the man who left sharpshooters' medals was in league with the Vietnamese. So far, though, he had no idea where to find him, no idea even where to start looking. All he could think of was to try to flush him out by hurting his gook friends.

That was Pardo's way of thinking. That was how he always thought and always operated—if you couldn't get to the man you wanted, then you went after his family, his friends, anybody he might come out to protect. Then, when he did, you got him.

It worked. It was part of the code of *la hombría*.

The point was to bring the sharpshooter out when you were ready for him. Which they had not been this afternoon at Tudor City. Who could have guessed that the sharpshooter would have been there, talking with old Brown Cao when the hitters came screaming on their cycles?

No one could have guessed, and if he hadn't been there, the hitters would have taken out Cao. The way he, Pardo, had personally taken out the old fool they called honored one.

Pardo's telephone rang. An hysterical woman on the line told him the sharpshooter had attacked Casino Bolívar. He'd killed José Goya, for one, plus many others, including Juan Llorente's bodyguards. Maybe even Llorente himself.

Pardo's thoughts raced. If the sharpshooter had knocked off Llorente, then who took over his authority?

He shelved the thought for later. For tonight, the war went on.

FOR THE WARRIOR it never ended, not tonight or any other night.

Doctorow had gone to Central Park, O'Brien said. It wasn't a bad idea for a narc on Saturday night. The dealers worked there, dealing to the runners who insisted on running in the park after midnight. The obsessive runners seemed not to care that both men and women runners, alone and in groups, had been attacked, not just by roving gangs of teenage hoodlums but also by junkies looking for the price of a pop.

Only the previous week a young copywriter for a major ad agency had been murdered while running after midnight in Central Park. And for what? His killer had wanted his expensive running shoes. That was all. A pair of shoes.

To say that the park became a jungle after dark was to understate the facts wildly. Jungle beasts killed for food. But these were different appetites.

The police patrolled the place a variety of ways. In cars, on horses, on foot. But Central Park was fifty blocks long. Inside the park were long stretches of open land skirted by lakes and ponds, shaded by woods and groves and traversed by rocky hills. Two hundred officers would not have been enough to cover the place after dark, and the city could not afford to put a quarter of that many there.

O'Brien had indicated that Bolan's best chance of finding Doctorow was likely to be in the northwest corner of Central Park, west of a pond called Harlem Mere. The streets around were not bad or dangerous, O'Brien said—it was the neighborhood called Morningside Heights and Columbia University was only a few blocks from the park—but even an armed narc had better be careful in that part of the park after midnight.

Bolan walked into Central Park a little before two in the morning.

It was as O'Brien had described it: busy, even at that hour. New Yorkers refused to allow the park to be closed at night, particularly in the summer.

People sat on the grass, eating and drinking at hilarious midnight picnics. The smell of charcoal grills was on the air. Grim runners sweated along the roads. The lights of the city reflected off the dark water.

He walked off the road, out into the open land called the North Meadow.

The scene was a little different. No parties on the grass. But there was huffing and grunting in the bushes, and the dealers would crop up occasionally. Colombians and Vietnamese, as if there were a truce.

Bolan walked on, looking for Doctorow, but saw no trace of him.

He walked on south, toward the reservoir, the largest body of water in the park. And he moved east. He moved into a part of Central Park darker than most areas, yet traversed with walks and bridle paths.

In a few minutes he was ready to swing back north toward a spot where Doc Doctorow was more likely to be.

Then he heard something. A whimper of protest? A moan?

Bolan trotted across the grass toward a little thicket. That was where he thought he'd heard the sound.

He was right. There she was. Barely visible in the dark, but on her back on the ground, with her running shorts pulled down around her knees.

A guy was on all fours a little distance from her. He was shaking his head, trying to recover his senses, from the look of him.

And standing around them was . . . trouble.

Four of them. No, five. A mixture of white and black. One he couldn't be sure. All tanked or high on something. They spoke Spanish, and Bolan understood enough to know they were talking about which one of them was going to have her first.

She understood, too, and gasped.

They laughed at her, then one of them turned and gave the guy on his hands and knees a kick alongside the head. That quieted him. He rolled over in the grass and groaned.

The winner of the argument—he looked the biggest and toughest—pulled down his pants and stood spread-eagled above the girl, showing her his pride.

When she sobbed hysterically, he stepped back a pace and bent his knees to kneel over her.

None of them had guessed there was an avenger nearby. They learned when the toe of a boot drove hard into the crotch of the one with his pants down.

Screaming in agony, the rapist threw himself on the ground, yelling and retching, clutching the parts that would not torment any girl tonight—and maybe no girl, any time, ever.

Bolan was alerted to the whispered sound of a long, thin knife coming out of its sheath. He swung around. A kick like a jackhammer impacted the knife wielder's shin, tearing away skin. The man yelled, but he was cut short by the massive fist that crushed his nose flat into his face.

A third guy launched himself into a karate stance and threatened with hands ready to chop. With his left fist Bolan drove one of those hands back against the guy's face. Then he hammered his right into the karate chopper's belly.

Three down.

The other two ran. But one of them wasn't fast enough to escape a swift, powerful kick in the backside that threw him headlong to the ground.

The girl, who had got up on her hands and knees while Bolan was cutting down her tormentors, crawled to the man who had just sprawled on the ground. As he rose, she swung at his face with a fist-sized rock. It crashed into his cheekbone, and Bolan could hear the bone break.

She moved with her rock to the one with his pants down. She raised the rock over her head and brought it down on the back of his neck.

"Hold it," Bolan said gently. "In this town you're apt to be the one that winds up in trouble, while these guys get off free."

She crawled to the young man who had been her companion when she came jogging in the park. She called his name brokenly, and he answered. He was not badly hurt.

She stood up again shakily, looking for the man who had rescued her. He'd earned her deepest gratitude and she wanted to thank him, but he was already gone.

FRANCISCO PARDO LED three men along East Eighth Street. Although there were some abandoned buildings in the neighborhood, which were occupied by squatters, most of the apartment buildings were in good repair, some of them even luxurious. The Vietnamese who lived in one of these buildings supposed no one knew they were even there.

That is, they supposed the brothers of *la hombría* didn't know they were there.

But Pardo knew. He had had men following the Vietnamese dealers for weeks. If they were going to be hit, they had to be hit where it hurt—where they had their wives and children, where they sheltered the graybeards they held in such esteem.

It was a simple operation. Pardo was carrying a bundle of dynamite sticks bound into a bomb with electrical tape. He knew how to handle dynamite. His bomb had two fuses, each one crimped into a copper cylinder, the detonator cap. Redundant, as the Yanquis said. If one fuse went out, the other would set off the charge.

One man walked up to the door with him. A glass door. Pardo used a cigar lighter to light the fuses. He nodded to the man, and the man blew away the glass with a short burst from his Uzi. Pardo threw the dynamite bomb into the hallway of the apartment building.

He had cut the fuses long enough to give them time to trot away but short enough so the bomb would explode before anyone could possibly pick it up and throw it out on the street.

He and his men were half a block away before the fiery explosion shot the front of the building across Eighth Street. The roof jumped, then fell down through the apartments. Then the building, along with the structures on either side of it, slowly collapsed.

7

The Zum Zum was open all night. It was one of a string of restaurants where a man could sit at the counter at four in the morning and eat a bowl of chili, a hot dog, a burger and fries, or if he was ready for breakfast, ham and eggs, bacon with pancakes and cup after cup of strong black coffee.

All kinds of people came in. No one who wasn't serious. The men and women who came into Zum Zum at four in the morning had worked all night or were about to go out and work a long day. They sat at the counter, hunched over their food, and ate hungrily—wearing clothes that told what they had done all night or would do all day.

Several languages were spoken. Spanish. Italian. A kind of English that was special to them and unknown anywhere else.

Three men sat at the counter early in the morning, nursing their cups of coffee.

Mack Bolan was still strong and alert after a long day and night, but was beginning to feel the effects of many waking hours and much work. Next to him was Doc and Captain Francis O'Brien, who had been awakened out of a sound sleep by the night's alarms.

"Civilians," O'Brien grumbled. "Six dead, and of those six only two were Vietnamese. Another day of this, and the mayor will call for troops." He shrugged. "Much good may it do him. If there were ten thousand soldiers in the five boroughs, they couldn't hold the lid on."

"Who are the chiefs?" asked Bolan. "Who's responsible?"

O'Brien shrugged again. "We can't prove. But we know. Like we know who the godfathers are. We don't have the evidence to go for indictments, but we know who should be indicted."

"So give," Bolan said.

O'Brien glanced at Doctorow. "It's embarrassing. The top guy among the Vietnamese is still thought of as a big hero in Washington."

"Air Marshal Diem?" asked Bolan.

"You got it," said O'Brien. "We'd like to see the son of a bitch deported, but there are senators who'd scream to high heaven."

"It's not just narcotics he's in," Doctorow supplied. "Marshal Le Xuan Diem sees himself as the crime boss of New York within five years."

"One of their big boys was killed Thursday night in the attack on Papillon," said Doctorow. "Vgo Nguyen Minh. His crowd are the chief suppliers of sotty. They make it somewhere in town, but we're not sure where. I think if we could find that lab, we'd take it out, legally or otherwise. Just take it out."

"Who would be running the lab, if Minh is gone?" Bolan asked.

"When he came to the States, he brought half a dozen young boys with him," said Doctorow. "Don't ask why. They've grown up, and most of them were still working for him when he was killed. We've heard two names, but neither of them has ever been arrested, so we don't know what they look like. One is called Pete, and one is called Bob. It's Pete Nhu and Bob Lac, so we hear. Couple of shady characters. You can be sure they're behind what's been happening this weekend."

"Among the Colombians," O'Brien elaborated, "the head guy is the man whose name you used last night. Juan Llorente. One of the guys you killed last night was also a big dealer. José Goya. His brother was a dealer, too, only smaller. He bought it in the attack on the building on 146th Street.''

"Both sides have got plenty of troops," Doctorow warned.

"Plus weapons, plus the guts to use them," O'Brien added. "We've got war in the streets."

Bolan looked at his companions quizzically. "Time to go after their generals," he said.

QUANT CHANH THANG SAT at the window of his apartment, which offered him a view of the East River, and pondered his problem.

How to find Bolan?

The man was a soldier. One of the best. Maybe the best Major Thang had ever seen. Brave...yes, but a lot more than brave. He was smart. Shrewd. Half a million dollars to kill him? The job would be worth every nickel.

The only advantage Thang had was that Bolan did not know he was no longer a brave soldier of the Republic of Vietnam, but was now a soldier in a very different army. Since Bolan did not know that, maybe he could be lured out to meet an old comrade-in-arms.

The question was how to contact him, Thang mused.

Surely there was a way—the way that had always brought Bolan onto the scene. Driven by his sense of justice, he would come where the animals were loose.

Fortunately Marshal Diem and Major Thang had animals at their disposal. He picked up the telephone and punched in Diem's number.

BOLAN GOT a few hours' sleep that Sunday morning. By a little after nine he was out on the streets, taking up the hunt again.

Even on a Sunday morning, the dealers were out. Not in Wall Street, which was deserted, but where New Yorkers went on a hot summer day—the beaches.

Bolan carried a red nylon bag—the kind men took to the beach to carry their trunks and towels, probably some tanning oil, and maybe a camera. He had stuffed two hotel towels into it. The Beretta 93-R was inside the middle compartment of the bag. In one of the other compartments he carried his extra ammo. The bag looked innocent, but it concealed what he needed.

The Atlantic rolled up on the sand, driven by a steady wind and breakers just powerful enough to exhilarate the swimmers but not strong enough to be dangerous. The sun gleamed on acres of oiled skin. Kids. Families. Young mothers exposing as much as they dared in bright-colored bikinis, and teenage girls going all out. Jocks flipping Frisbees or tossing footballs.

Tantalizing and familiar smells floated in the air. Hot dogs. The real Coney Island hots, not to be found anywhere else in the world. Gallons of mustard and relish. Hamburgers. Pizza slices. Enough beer to float a ship. There were rivers of sodas, as New Yorkers called all kinds of soft drinks. Mamas presided over huge picnic hampers and pulled out more kinds of homemade food than Bolan could name.

Vendors sold their wares. Including grass, coke, sotty.

The less-wholesome goods were sold, if not actually openly, then with not a great deal of subtlety. But under the eyes of cops who knew what was going on and hadn't been paid off—who just knew the futility of busting guys who would be back on the streets with their stuff in two or three hours. A cop's job here was simply to keep the dealers from shooting.

The Executioner walked along the boardwalk, checking out the dealers.

There was some kind of truce apparently. Colombians sold crack, and Vietnamese sold sotty, all within a few yards. They didn't so much as glare at the competition.

There were even some guys selling other stuff—heroin, pills—and some flamboyant but threadbare blacks selling grass, all working the same crowd and not getting in each other's way.

Coney Island on Sunday afternoon was a supermarket of substances.

Bolan walked up to a Colombian, an olive-skinned man carrying his merchandise in a small beach bag.

"What ya got, buddy?"

"Happy dust," said the Latin American, showing gold teeth in his smile. "Top quality. No flour. No bug poison."

"I been known to waste guys who sold me the wrong stuff," said Bolan.

The dealer did just what Bolan had hoped he would do— shifted his eyes to a man standing watchfully some ten yards away. That identified the legbreaker for Bolan. The second Colombian stepped a few paces nearer.

Made bolder by his legbreaker, the dealer stared hard into Bolan's face. "You want the happy dust, smart man? Or no?"

Bolan reached into his pocket, took out a sharpshooter's medal and casually handed it over.

The Colombian blanched. He turned to the legbreaker and showed him what the big American had handed him.

The legbreaker came up to Bolan. "We want no trouble," he said. "What you want?"

"Let's take a little walk down the beach to the water," Bolan suggested. "The three of us."

"So, okay."

They stepped down from the boardwalk and walked across the beach, among the press of oiled bodies basking in the bright sunlight. They had to step over outstretched legs, sometimes on the edges of beach towels and blankets, but no one particularly noticed them, except for a pair of teenage girls in microscopic bikinis who sized up Bolan and smiled invitingly at him.

The three men reached the edge of the surf.

"What now, boss?" asked the legbreaker.

"Open the bag," said Bolan, nodding at the beach bag containing the dealer's stock-in-trade.

"Hey..." the dealer started to say. One look at the grim face of the big man who handed out sharpshooters' medals changed his mind. He kept silent and opened the bag. It contained envelopes of cocaine and vials of crack.

"One by one," Bolan ordered. "Tear 'em up and dump the stuff on the sand where the waves will come up."

"Hey, man," the legbreaker protested. "You got any idea how much money that stuff's worth? Can't we make a deal?"

"Like what?" Bolan asked coldly.

"We give you the money that's in the bag. Or the money and some of the stuff."

Bolan shook his head. He pointed at the bag, then at the sand.

The dealer reached into the bag, pulled out a little envelope, tore it open and poured white powder into the water.

"You do that one at a time, it's gonna take all day," said Bolan. "So get to it. Both of you. *Now!*"

A small crowd gathered and watched curiously as the two men ripped the envelopes, broke open the vials and poured—first cocaine, then rocks of crack—onto the sand, where Bolan ground the stuff under his boots before the waves rushed up the beach and carried it away.

"You're pollutin' the ocean," chided a tall blonde in a yellow bikini.

Twenty yards away, a policeman stood, watching with interest, not moving.

The blonde gave a giddy little laugh and nudged Bolan with an elbow. "Gawd! Like the stuff was going out of style! You some new kind of narc, buddy?"

"Yeah," said Bolan. "War on drugs. New style."

"Well, good luck to ya," said a fat man with an unlit cigar in his mouth.

Bolan let the dealer and legbreaker keep the money. He didn't want it for himself, and having them throw it in the water might have caused a riot. He let them trudge back up the beach.

The crowd quickly lost interest, except for the blonde in the yellow bikini. "The name is Deirdre."

"Hi," said Bolan.

It would have been easy to want to know her better. The blond hair wasn't meant to look like nature's own color and tumbled down her back in provocative disarray. She had a figure that would fix any man's attention.

"You gonna tell me your name?"

"Sorry. It's Mike."

"Okay, Mike. Hang on a minute. I want to show you something."

She reached into a small, white, knitted bag and pulled out a leather card case. He knew what was in there; he'd seen them before. He stared at her shield and her ID—Detective Lieutenant Deirdre Levantis, NYPD.

"What's the deal, Mike...or whatever your name is?"

"Kid brother got hung up on that stuff. Ruined his life. Makes me mad."

"What you did didn't do any good," she said. "They'll pick up another supply and be back in business in half an hour. And if you go near that pair again, somebody'll kill you. Besides that, there are fifty of them working the area. I could've busted that pair. But what the hell? If I don't see them pushing it to kids—" She shrugged.

"Thanks for the advice," he said.

He started to edge away from her, but she moved with him.

"I wanna know somethin'," she said. "How you managed to get them to do it. You just stood there, and they threw away—what?—a hundred thousand bucks' worth of crack and coke. Why? Just who the hell are you?"

"Do you object to what I did?"

"Hell, no."

"Then why don't you leave it alone?"

"For starters, you're gonna get yourself killed. C'mon, big guy, you can't start a one-man war on the biggest business in town. Those guys play rough."

The Executioner nodded. "I'll be careful," he said.

"I suggest you beat it out of here," she said. "They'll be looking for you."

He nodded again. "Thanks," he said with a quick wave of his hand. Then he walked away from her, up the beach, while she stood with her feet in the surf and gazed after him.

Bolan returned to the boardwalk. He passed by a dozen other dealers working the crowds, hating to see the amount of business they did. He could have stopped any one of them, but as the blond cop had pointed out, there wasn't much point in stopping any one of them.

He picked out another one to receive a sharpshooter's medal, this time a Vietnamese dealing sotty.

"Don't I know you from somewhere?" he asked the Viet boy—for this dealer was no more than twenty years old.

"No, you don't know me, and I don't know you," the boy said.

"Back in Nam."

The dealer sneered. "I left there when I was five years old. You think maybe you're my father? That's possible, if you were GI. You want some good stuff, daddy? I deal in the best, only the best."

Just like the Colombian, the dealer shifted his eyes to his enforcer, and true to form, the legbreaker stepped closer.

"Let me show you something," Bolan said, including the legbreaker with a look as he pulled a medal from his pocket and pressed it into the hand of the young dealer.

"What's this shit, man? What you doin', sellin' your medals for a pop each? No, thanks. Hand me ten bucks. You can keep the medal. I don't need no more souvenirs."

The legbreaker reached for the medal. He took it and stared at it for a moment, then nodded.

Bolan felt the point of a knife in the small of his back. This dealer was working with two legbreakers, and one had moved in from behind.

"Gotcha," said the first one. "You ain't so smart after all. They said you was smart."

Bolan shot his left fist into the face of the first leg-breaker, throwing his body forward just enough to break the contact between the point of the knife and the skin of his back. And quickly, very quickly, he jammed his right elbow back at the man behind him.

He couldn't see the legbreaker behind or tell where he'd hit him, but he felt hard contact as if he'd hit him in the ribs, and he heard the man huff in surprise and pain.

Knowing the man wasn't hurt enough to be stopped from using the knife, Bolan threw himself to one side. The knife struck under his left arm. He felt the cut like the touch of a hot iron.

He spun around. The man lunged to stab again. Bolan chopped him across the bridge of the nose and felt the nose crunch in. Blood sprayed into the air, but the man threw himself desperately toward the warrior, the knife out in front of him.

Bolan stepped aside, and as the man lunged past, chopped him across the back of the neck. The Vietnamese dropped.

The first legbreaker had recovered a little and was staggering to the attack with a knife. Bolan sidestepped a thrust and smashed the man's jaw with a hard left.

The young dealer stood gaping, afraid to move.

"Okay," said Bolan. "You got the medal. Give me the stuff. I mean the bag. Give me the bag."

A crowd had congregated around the fight—a much bigger crowd than had gathered at the edge of the water. Every man and woman kept a cautious distance. They stared, but none of them moved to help.

Bolan knew he was bleeding. The knife had not entered deep, but he was hurt. With the bag of sotty in hand, he stalked through the crowd.

No one offered to help. But one man said, "Buddy, I wouldn't give much for the chance of a guy that did what you just did."

Bolan went into the first public rest room he found. He tossed rocks of sotty into one ceramic fixture after another, down the line, flushing them as he went, until all the stuff was gone. The dealer's cash followed the same route.

Inside one of the stalls he opened his beach bag, unwrapped the Desert Eagle and used the towel as a temporary bandage to hold back the blood. He put his shirt back on over the towel, even though it was bloodstained, and he pressed his left elbow to his side to hold the towel in place.

He went back out onto the boardwalk. The crowd that had assembled to watch the fight had dispersed. None of the Vietnamese was in sight.

"Big guy, you're gonna get yourself wasted."

He turned toward the voice. It was Deirdre Levantis. She had thrown a terry cloth beach coat over her bikini, and she had put on sandals.

"You don't miss much, do you?" said Bolan.

She reached into her bag and pulled out a small pair of binoculars. "I watched you. I figured you're not the kinda guy that takes advice. I also figured out you're not just some dummy who thinks he can make a dent in the trade. And right now you need some help. C'mon. I'll take you where we can do something about that knife wound."

"Hospital . . . ?" he asked skeptically, shaking his head.

Deirdre shrugged. "What makes me think the last thing you want is to see a doc and have a report filed that a guy with a knife wound came in? We'll go someplace where we can have a look at it. If it requires a hospital, that's what you'll get, ol' buddy. If not . . . we'll see."

"This official?" he asked.

"Not if you don't act like an idiot."

SHE LIVED IN BENSONHURST, in a tiny apartment locked with four locks, cooled by two roaring air conditioners. Together they stripped off his bloody shirt and unwrapped the towel from around his body. The dried blood stuck the towel to his wound, and it came away painfully. But the wound was not deep, not threatening. She applied a first-aid ointment and thick gauze pads to serve as pressure bandages.

"Drink it," she said as she handed him a Scotch and soda, "whether you like it or not. So what *is* this crap?"

He sipped from the drink she had pushed into his hands. "How does a guy tell a policewoman to mind her own business?" he asked. "It's your business. I know it's your business. But take my word for it, Deirdre . . . you should back away from this one."

She tipped her head and looked at him, her face showing mixed amusement and disbelief. She had tossed off the beach coat and was again quite bare in her little yellow bikini. Deirdre was, beyond any argument, a striking woman—dark brown eyes contrasting nicely with her bleached-blond hair, long shapely legs, leading the eye upward to a generous bosom.

"I been a cop eight years," she said. "Detective five of those years, assigned to narcotics. I got an idea I know who you are. But I know you won't tell me, so I won't ask. So never mind. But you hit the Colombians today and then the Vietnamese. Mister, those guys know how to hate."

"That was the idea," he said.

"And you like to work alone."

"I always have."

"What would you do if I tried to put you under arrest for the unlicensed pistols you're carrying in that bag?"

He shrugged.

"So don't try to get rid of me, big guy. I got a fire in my own gut about what you were challenging today. And I'm willing to work independent. Okay? You can't work alone in the Big Apple. You don't know it well enough. I won't call me a partner, but if you're Batman, I'm gonna be Robin a while. Deal? You're stuck with me, anyway."

MARSHAL LE XUAM DIEM PUT down the telephone. He turned to Major Quant Chanh Thang. "It is him. He confronts and overwhelms three good men, in public, without using a weapon. He walks off with a hundred thousand dollars' worth of merchandise and money and—and mark this well—*flushes them down the toilets* in a public rest room. No one else. No one else would want to, and no one else would dare."

"But this time," said Major Thang, "we know where he has gone."

"What?"

"He was wounded," Thang explained. "Our observers saw him bleeding from a knife wound. He left bloody paper towels in the men's room where he flushed the merchandise down the toilets. And outside . . . Outside he was met by a NYPD detective, who took him away in her car.

"A female detective by the name of Levantis. Narcotics detail. Plainclothes. I should say, *very* plain clothes. She was waiting outside the rest rooms when he came out."

"You plan, then, to earn your half-million dollars by—"

Major Thang smiled. "By blasting Mr. Bolan and his Detective Levantis into oblivion."

"And the animals?"

"Let us cage the animals for a while. I will send an engineer this time."

"A MAN WHO HAS LOST BLOOD needs to keep his strength up," Deirdre Levantis said playfully as they lay together in her bed.

Bolan smiled lazily. What they'd had together had been perfect, perfectly performed and perfectly understood: something between a man and a woman who were hungry for what they could give each other but knew there could be no commitment between them, nothing that would last longer than this afternoon's joy.

"A guy needs *something* to recover his strength," Bolan chuckled.

"Besides, who knows, there could be another round," she said.

"What you got in mind?"

"Thick rare steak," she said. "Fries. Everything we're not supposed to eat."

"Got to go to my hotel first," he said. "Clothes—"

"The place I've got in mind, you don't need a shirt and tie."

"Don't think I could go in a shirt ripped open with a knife and stained with blood."

"You made your point," she said. "Hotel first. Then Brighton Beach and a place I know where they graze the cows right in the backyard so the steaks practically moo on your plate."

He wore a black T-shirt of hers, stretched over him until the seams were ready to break. She pulled on tight blue jeans and a yellow T-shirt with a slogan printed on it—I ♥ NY.

She had laughed when she compared the weapons they were carrying—her snub-nosed police .38 in her little handbag, the Beretta and Eagle in his beach bag. She had laughed, that is, until she took a closer look at his two handguns. Then she had shaken her head. "A pro," she'd said. "Just what I figured."

Their weapons accompanied them as they went down the stairs in the two-story apartment building. Neither of them was ever off duty.

"Car belong to the city of New York?' he asked as they walked toward her four-year-old battered blue Ford.

She looked up and grinned. "Would *I* own a heap like that?" she asked.

She deserved decent treatment, so he walked around the car to the driver's side, and when she unlocked the door, he opened it for her.

She flung herself energetically behind the wheel. As he walked around the rear of the car, she put her key in the ignition and turned it to start the engine.

The explosion threw Bolan to the sidewalk. By the time he staggered to his feet, the smoke and fire had subsided. The charge had been set under the front seat, and the gas tank hadn't blown. The Ford was torn apart.

And so was Deirdre.

There was no point in yelling. No point in staggering around the car, reaching for her. There was no more Deirdre.

The heavy sense of responsibility had just started to feel like a lead weight in his stomach when he realized it was a luxury he couldn't afford.

A slug punched into the shattered Ford, missing him by inches.

Bolan swung around, dropping into a crouch in the same movement. He spotted the shooter, a slight-looking Vietnamese, taking aim.

Beretta, hell! Quiet kill, hell! He pulled the Desert Eagle from his beach bag, swung the muzzle toward the Vietnamese—who had the boldness to be trotting toward him—and blew him off his feet with one quick shot that severed his spine.

Two more men popped into view with their Mini-Uzis. The machine pistols barked and bucked, and two streams of 9 mm slugs kicked off the pavement and shook the Ford.

Bolan threw himself over the hood of the wreck and gained a little shelter.

The Vietnamese seemed to think they could just blow the whole world away with the amazing firepower of their Uzis, which suggested they had little or no experience with such weapons. They let fly more streams of slugs . . . and both of them ran out of ammo at the same time.

They fumbled nervously with magazines. They began to back away fearfully.

In other circumstances the executioner might have let them run. But not now. He stepped out from behind the wreckage of the Ford. His first shot from the Eagle threw one of the Vietnamese on his back, his body blown open by the .44 Mag slug.

The other struggled to press his clip into place so he could raise his muzzle and open fire. But he never had the chance. Bolan's .44 Mag slug tore off the arm that held the gun, and the man dropped to his knees, shrieking. He would bleed to death before anyone could help him.

Bolan glanced one last time at the Ford, then strode away before the first unit from NYPD arrived.

THE CABBIE GLANCED apprehensively into the back seat. The man sitting there seemed tightly coiled, like a cobra ready to strike. A particular kind of frozen hell burned from his eyes, and the driver decided it might be just as well if he forgot this fare. If someone asked, he had delivered a woman and two kids to the beach on this run.

Bolan walked along the boardwalk. Just the way Deirdre had predicted, the guys he'd ripped off that afternoon were there again.

They began to walk away backward when they saw him.

"Okay," he said. "Who fingered the girl?"

The young dealer smirked. "You're a dead man, smart guy," he said. "Sure. One phone call. You're supposed to be the dead one, but she'll do. You... It's just a question of time. You stuck your nose in the wrong business this time."

Bolan turned to the enforcers. "You got the idea straight? You understand enough to report it back?"

The one who'd put the knife in Bolan's back shook his head. "Didn't know who you were, man. Swear to God!"

"*He* fingered the girl?"

The enforcer shrugged. "Wasn't me," he said.

"Wasn't me, either," said the other one.

"Your friends don't seem a whole lot interested in saving your ass," Bolan pointed out.

"Soldiers," said the boy scornfully. "Expendable. Aren't they always expendable, soldiers? When you were in—"

"You and I are going for a walk," Bolan said.

The dealer tried to play it cool. "Figures," he said. "Big man, aren't you?"

Bolan glanced at the two legbreakers. "Okay with you guys?"

"So long as he doesn't live to complain about it," one of them hurried to say.

Bolan nodded. He jerked his head toward the dealer. "Move."

"Where we goin'?"

"We're gonna find out what your stuff is good for," said Bolan.

He herded the dealer to another public men's room farther along on the boardwalk. Bolan shoved him inside and into the room of stalls, which was deserted.

"Look at this," said Bolan, showing the Beretta. "Silent. Subsonic. I can put a slug between your ribs, and a guy standing six feet away will wonder why you fell over. So...sit." He pointed with the gun.

There were no doors on the toilet stalls. The dealer stepped inside one and sat down. He eyed the Beretta solemnly.

"You eat what you sell," Bolan ordered coldly. "Let's see if it makes you sick."

"*Sick!* Man, it—"

"Which never bothered you when you sold it to other people," said Bolan.

"Hey, man! Sotty is supposed to be *smoked!*"

"You got a pipe?"

"No!"

"Make yourself two cigarettes of it...there must be some rolling paper in your pocket—for emergencies."

"Shit! Man, you—"

"Or a quiet slug in the balls, and I'll go home and leave you here."

The dealer kept protesting that he didn't have any papers for making a cigarette, but under Bolan's cold threat, he reluctantly pulled some from his pocket. He laid three rocks in line on the harsh toilet paper of the public toilet and slowly rolled a tube that was more like a cigar than a cigarette.

He claimed he didn't have a match, but Bolan made him empty his pocket, and a book of paper matches fell to the floor.

The dealer cast a pleading glance at Bolan. He no longer seemed cocky and brazen.

"What you worried about? It's only what you sell other people to smoke."

"Aw . . . *Gawd!*" the dealer croaked after he had puffed a little on the burning paper and sotty.

"Keep at it," said Bolan. "Still better than a slug in the balls, don't you figure?"

The Vietnamese smoked on, his face twisted with anxiety, but in a little while he stopped protesting. The narcotic euphoria overwhelmed him. He smoked hungrily, and when he had finished the first cigar, he eagerly accepted the second.

Ten minutes later Bolan left the men's room. The Vietnamese dealer lay facedown on the tiled floor. His survival depended on somebody calling the emergency medical service—unless he was taken for just one more passed-out junkie and allowed to lie there.

Mack Bolan didn't really care. .

8

The main sotty lab was in a building on White Street, a crosstown street not far north of city hall, not far north of the Brooklyn Bridge. It was a street of aging brick buildings, some of which were being sandblasted and remodeled into choice apartments, while others still housed businesses.

The sotty lab was in one of the smaller and still-not-remodeled buildings just east of Broadway, occupying a big room on the back of the third floor.

The rest of the building was leased in the name of Nhu & Company, carpet cleaners. Pete Nhu did in fact operate a carpet-cleaning service out of the first floor. His vans, coming into White Street with big cans of chemicals, looked innocent to neighbors, who were not very anxious in any case to know what went on in any of the buildings on the block. They really didn't want to know that the big cans supposed to be full of cleaning fluids were really filled with ethyl ether and acetone, the highly flammable—actually explosive—chemicals used in the process of turning cocaine into rocks of crack.

No one noticed, either, the crates of weapons that were carried in from the street. They were overlooked in the traffic of rolled rugs and cleaning supplies.

The second floor was the arsenal.

There also was the dormitory and kitchen for the Vietnamese girls who worked for Pete Nhu. Most of them were illegal aliens, and no one noticed that, either. They barely spoke English. They considered themselves lucky to be in the States, even if they were little better than slaves to the man who had brought them here. They were well fed, well dressed, and they watched American television and learned English and looked forward to the day when they would become legals. Then they could find husbands and live in country homes with trees and swimming pools, and their children would go to the palaces Americans built for schools. They went out infrequently and only in the company of a man or an older woman. Their entertainment consisted of outings to baseball games or to movies in huge theaters. Sometimes they were driven to the beaches in the state of New Jersey, where they splashed in the surf and promised each other that their someday homes would be near the beaches.

Pete Nhu had other girls, but not in the building on White Street. The very prettiest ones were offered the opportunity to make a lot of money fast, as prostitutes. They lived in apartments uptown and earned eight times what they were paid and were happy with that pay and thought the man who arranged this life for them was a generous benefactor.

How to do all this, and more, Pete Nhu had learned from Vgo Nguyen Minh, the honored one, but the honored one had known little, almost nothing, of what his "son" Nhu had achieved. Pete Nhu figured he had paid his dues to the honored one many times over. Bob Lac hadn't quite seen it that way, but Bob Lac had his enterprises, too.

The building on White Street was one more thing to Nhu. It was his home. On the third floor, in a suite of magnificently furnished rooms at the front of the building, Pete Nhu kept a residence the honored one had never suspected.

It was in the bedroom of his lavish apartment that Pete Nhu awakened late, feeling comfortable and lazy.

Brown Cao had missed yesterday. He hadn't taken out the man who distributed sharpshooters' medals. But he'd come close, and more to the point, he hadn't been identified and hadn't lost his value.

What was more, he hadn't been paid.

Nhu smelled coffee. He was pleased that Dinh My Linh had learned to make good coffee. She was also learning English, so they could talk better. And, though she was only fifteen, she had learned womanly arts some women didn't learn ever, or if they did, they learned them only ten or twenty years later.

She came in, bearing a tray with tiny cups and the pot of coffee. She wore only a loose silk shift, with no undergarments beneath it, and her delicate little feet were bare. That was his rule for her—that she go without shoes or undergarments inside the apartment. Only when he took her out was she fully clothed, and then she delighted in the exquisite and expensive things he bought for her.

It was obvious to Pete Nhu that Dinh My Linh was happy. She remembered nothing of life in the old country, which she had left as an infant with her parents. They had been boat people. Her father was now one of the shrimp fisherman working off the Texas coast. He and her mother had sold Dinh My Linh to Pete Nhu for the money that bought their shrimp boat, free and clear. The rest of the family lived well off the proceeds from the sale of this one daughter. If she hadn't been happy, they wouldn't have wanted to know it, and if she wasn't, she wouldn't want them to know it.

He called her Mia, and she thought it a compliment and loved it.

"Ees pretty morning, no?" she said.

"*'Is,'* Mia. "Not 'ees.'"

She nodded. "'Is.' It...is...a...pretty morning. Yes?"

Pete Nhu nodded and grinned. "It is a pretty morning, Mia. A Monday morning." He sighed. "A morning when I must go out and fight against those who would destroy us again, Mia. Even here."

"Yes...*Pete*," she said hesitantly. She found it difficult to use his American name.

Pete Nhu drank the coffee she had brought him and quickly dressed. He kissed her on the cheek before he left the apartment to go out to command his enterprises.

Dinh My Linh stood at the window of the living room of the luxuriously furnished apartment and watched Pete Nhu walk out to an inconspicuous car and be taken away. She pulled on panties and slipped her feet into sneakers. When he came home, she had to be bathed and scented with the expensive perfume he bought her, but she didn't have to follow any of his whims when she was alone. Alone, she was a *person,* not a girl her father had sold to a criminal.

BOLAN SAT ASTRIDE a motorcycle, wearing leathers and a helmet. Half a block away, Doc Doctorow sat behind the wheel of an unmarked car.

"Check the Porsche," said Doctorow.

"Got it," Bolan answered.

They communicated by radio. Bolan's radio was in the helmet. The microphone fastened to his throat and covered by a silk scarf was voice activated. Whatever he said, Doctorow heard it.

The leathers were hot, and he was sweating inside them. They made good cover for his two holsters and two pistols, though. The bike was a beast, a BMW motorcycle—big, heavy, heavy powered. It had once been used to carry crack to dealers, and when the courier was busted, the bike was confiscated under federal law.

Actually the black leathers had also been confiscated. That was the law—anything used in the narcotics trade was forfeit. As a result, the DEA had some fine cars and even a speedboat here in New York.

The red Porsche was a 911, one hell of a car. It sat squat and imposing on wide-set wheels, the air-cooled engine gurgling authoritatively in the rear. The removable roof was off, leaving the car open between the wide stainless-steel bar and the windshield.

It had stopped beside a dealer. Maybe just to make a buy. Maybe to make a delivery.

It was a delivery. Bolan saw the briefcase handed in through the open roof and another one handed out. The dealer saluted as the Porsche swung away and turned onto Broadway.

Bolan gunned the bike and took off after it. He didn't need to look back to see if Doctorow was coming.

The idea was not to catch up with the Porsche. The idea was to follow it to the next guy up the line and maybe to the lab.

Bolan and Doctorow were to trade off, one keeping close while the other held back, then switch and do it the other way so the driver of the Porsche would not see he was being tailed.

It was difficult for the car, easier for the motorcycle, in the confused mid-morning traffic and tangled streets of lower Manhattan. The trade of briefcases had taken place just as Bolan had seen it on Friday, and on the same street. Having done a rich business in the past two hours, the Porsche was moving out of the financial district.

The Porsche's driver made an easy right turn off Broadway, passed to the east of city hall and then executed an abrupt turn into the ramp leading onto the Brooklyn Bridge. He sped across the bridge, weaving from one lane to another. Bolan followed, but he knew Doctorow had fallen hopelessly far behind.

The BMW bike was perfect for this chase. It's engine was powerful yet muffled and quiet, so that when he accelerated and shot through a hole in traffic, the bike did not roar and alert the driver of the Porsche.

Still, it was only a matter of time for the two men in the bright red Porsche to become aware that the big bike coming along behind them did not stay back there just as a coincidence.

THE MAN in the passenger seat of the red Porsche was Bob Lac. The car was equipped with a cellular telephone, and he picked it up and dialed a number.

"Bob. Coming down Adams Street toward borough hall. Got a BMW hog on our tail. We'll go Fulton. Get the son of a bitch."

THE FIRST TRY at getting the son of a bitch came at Fulton and Grand, where a battered white van ran a red light and put himself between the Porsche and Bolan on the bike.

Bolan shrieked into a left skid, leaving a trail of smoking rubber on the pavement, almost turned but righted the bike and lost only a hundred yards. He twisted in speed and cut the loss.

"Where the hell are you?" came Doctorow's voice.

Bolan spoke into the mike. "Somewhere in Brooklyn. I don't know the geography very well. Fulton Street. Okay. Going east. They got it figured, I think."

"Moving," said Doctorow. "Keep telling me where you are. I got little chance of catching up, but—"

The Porsche began to run traffic lights. It picked up a blue-and-white that roared away from the curb and pursued, siren screaming, lights flashing.

The problem for the blue-and-white was that the red car was a Porsche. The solid little sports car turned right, making the corner at forty-five miles an hour as level as if it had been going fifteen, accelerating out of the sharp turn and gaining distance from the blue-and-white. All the driver had to do was point the car where he wanted to go. The police Ford, at only thirty-five, skidded through the turn, swaying, back end coming around too far, tires howling, losing ground—only to see the Porsche turn left ahead, again without slowing.

Bolan, too, lost the Porsche. But he figured that east on Fulton meant something and that the Porsche would return to it. Sure enough, he saw it speed back onto Fulton, a block and a half ahead, and he put on more speed and shot after it.

The cops were no dummies, either. The blue-and-white roared back onto Fulton. Bolan could see it back there, red and blue lights flashing.

Only it was a long way back.

The Porsche swung left. Fulton was no good for them now. The cops on their radio would have units on it in a minute.

Bolan followed.

The chase took a zigzag course, through crowded neighborhood streets where people scrambled out of the way and stared after the little red car and the big bike.

Bolan tried to tell Doctorow where he was, but he could not read the signs and ride and keep the Porsche in sight, all at the same time.

"Piece of luck. He just sideswiped a van. Van's going on the sidewalk. Look out! Missed...missed a kid. But a pole's coming down. Tore a fender on the Porsche, I bet. Hasn't slowed him down. Now, he's working his way left. What's that? North? Hey! Cemetery! The whole world out here is one big cemetery!"

"Okay, buddy. I know where you are. Be there."

The red Porsche tore through a gate ahead and into one of the roads that ran through the big cemetery.

Then, as Bolan squeezed on the brakes and put the bike into a straight-ahead skid, the wrought-iron cemetery gate swung shut. And crouching on both sides were guys with what looked like Uzis. Ready to fire.

Bolan skidded the bike around and let go. He was thrown off as the bike skidded crazily, then turned over and tumbled toward the gunners.

He rolled on the pavement in his leathers. That was what they were for, to protect a man's hide when he went off a bike and hit the pavement.

The first burst of fire chopped into the bike, blowing tires. The gunners hadn't figured it out yet that the rider had separated from the bike.

That gave the warrior a moment to orient himself and draw the Desert Eagle.

Flat on his belly on the blacktop, he took aim and flopped a gunner—a man fool enough to stand with legs apart and challenge.

For a brief moment the chatter of fire stopped. The huge explosion from the Eagle and the quick death of one of their number changed everything quickly.

Some of them weren't even sure where the deadly shot had come from.

Bolan counted five of them. He took their moment of confusion to crawl backward and find himself some protection under the edge of the pavement, in a shallow drainage ditch.

They were Vietnamese. Young. He guessed none of them had much experience with the automatic weapons they carried. They knew how to menace with them, not to fire them.

That was apparent when they opened fire again. The fire—a great, roaring storm of it—passed over his head. It ricocheted off pavement, it tore up sod in the cemetery, blew showers of chips off monuments.

The Executioner aimed at the gunner whose fire was coming closest and banished him, along with his weapon, to silence. The Viet's gun flew in the air as he was thrown back by the .44 Magnum slug.

The remaining four crawled backward under a fence of heavy black chain, and emerged into the cemetery, taking shelter behind marble grave markers and monuments. From there they stuck out their Uzis and fired quick, short, useless bursts.

Still, the fire was heavy enough to prevent Bolan from moving.

They knew where he was now. Their fire was wild, but there was plenty of it. Bolan was pinned down.

Or was he?

Typical target range for the Mini-Uzi was twenty-one feet. A good marksman could drop a man reliably at that distance. These gunners, who obviously were not good marksmen, were at twice that distance. Bolan pondered for a moment, then jumped up and ran twenty yards to his left before throwing himself to the ground again, in a deeper place in the ditch, where it had better protection.

Stuttering fire followed him, but it was all over the place, nowhere close to hitting him.

What was more, they exhausted their magazines and began to fumble nervously, mounting new ones.

He got up and dashed back into the cemetery on his side of the road, taking cover behind a big block of marble carved into a monument.

It was time to move, to keep moving. Maybe the Vietnamese hadn't noticed, but the police were converging on the cemetery—at least three cars of them, sirens howling, horns hooting.

Bolan made his way among the tombstones, putting distance between him and the police.

The Vietnamese opened fire on the blue-and-whites as they careered into the cemetery. The cars spun around, officers jumped out and returned fire with their service pistols.

As Bolan maintained his pace, gaining more separation from what was developing into a full battle, he heard more cars coming. Also, he heard the deep boom of police shotguns.

"Where the hell are you?" asked Doctorow on the radio.

"How'm I supposed to know? In a big cemetery."

"'Nough said. I know where you are, about. Go east. I'll pick you up."

Bolan knelt on the ground and shed the motorcycle leathers, which left him dressed in blue jeans and a white T-shirt. He poured the dead flowers out of two plastic urns left on a pair of graves and used them to conceal the Desert Eagle and the Beretta, along with their holsters. He took the radio out of the helmet. A little distance away he saw a cemetery workman's abandoned shovel. He picked it up. Looking like a maintenance worker with a shovel and two empty urns, he strode east. He didn't really think they'd get their quarry this time, but there would be other chances. He'd make sure of that.

THE RED PORSCHE WAS speeding east on the Interborough Parkway. Bob Lac was talking on the cellular telephone.

"Cut it. Cut losses. Break it off and forget it."

The Porsche had been damaged when it sideswiped the van. The driver could still steer, but he could make no sharp left turns. When he tried, the left front tire rubbed torn metal.

"Cops," muttered the driver.

An NYPD blue-and-white that had been sitting on an exit ramp screamed after them. Lac turned around and saw the angry flashing lights.

He grabbed a sawed-off automatic shotgun from the black seat, stood up, thrusting his head and shoulders out through the open top of the car, and pointed the shotgun at the police car. The police driver saw what was coming and jammed on his brakes, but he was too late. Lac pulled the trigger twice, and a storm of buckshot dissolved the windshield of the police car and shredded the driver's face with glass and lead.

The blue-and-white hit the concrete center divider, glanced off, leaving a wheel behind, and turned around twice before it skidded from the pavement and into a retaining wall to the right.

"Off the parkway!" Lac yelled at the driver of the Porsche. "This car's hot!"

A few minutes later the two Vietnamese walked casually into a shopping center—two well-dressed men in dark suits and straw hats, carrying briefcases and looking like the kind of young men who were engaged in selling insurance policies, stocks or real estate. A few minutes later they found an unlocked station wagon with the keys in it, and they drove it back the way they had come, passing the wrecked police car and the three emergency vehicles around it, and on back to Manhattan.

QUANT CHANH THANG SAT at a desk in the New York offices of the Drug Enforcement Administration.

"Mr. Doctorow has not called in this morning, Major Thang," said the young woman who had agreed to receive the faintly mysterious Vietnamese. "All I can do, really, is give him your name and telephone number when he does call. I'm sorry I can't tell you when he will call, but it's in the nature of our work, you understand, that sometimes he is gone for days."

"I quite understand," said the major politely. "Let me leave my card."

Two hours later Doctorow dialed the number the major had left.

"It is kind of you to call, Mr. Doctorow," said Major Thang smoothly. "I know you must be very busy."

"A little," said Doctorow dryly.

"My reason for contacting you is a bit unusual," the major went on. "I think it is possible, just possible, that you and I have a mutual friend, and I am hoping you might be able to put me in touch with him."

"Who is that?"

"He has used various names. He and I were friends many years ago in Vietnam. I know he will remember. He was a soldier. A fine soldier. The best. But there was some trouble. I have heard of him occasionally over the years, and I understand that he has become active in the effort to stamp out the commerce in harmful substances. Since that is your field, too, and since there is so much activity in that area in the city these days, I thought it possible you might know of the man and might be able to give him my name."

"I don't think I know who you mean," said Doctorow.

"Yes, of course. He was always most discreet…and you would be, about him. All I ask is, if you happen to run across the man, mention my name and tell him I would like to meet him again sometime, to talk over old times. A pair of old soldiers with many fine memories. All right?"

"Yes. I understand. I don't think I know this man, but I will pass your name along to some other people. It's possible that someone might know him."

"I should be grateful."

"Okay. And what was his name, Major?"

"I knew him by the name of Bolan…Sergeant Bolan. He might remember me as Major Thing. Some Americans thought it was humorous to call me that."

"Well," Doctorow said, "I'll put the word around."

Doctorow put down the telephone. Bolan put down another one. He had been listening on an extension.

"Major Thing," said Bolan, frowning. "I *did* know him." He nodded. "Yeah, I knew him. A fine soldier."

"A trap," said Doctorow.

"Hard to believe," said Bolan. "I can't think that Major Quant Chanh Thang could—"

"Let me check him out," Doctorow offered. "I'll have the FBI check him. And NYPD."

Bolan nodded. "If he's legit, I *would* like to see him." He paced restlessly around, then paused before the window. "About the lab," he went on after a minute. "Maybe there's a better way to find it."

"Got to be," said Doctorow.

"The stuff comes in," said Bolan. "I mean, cocaine and heroin. It comes in through the airports. Off boats. It's also brought in by trucks. And you guys watch for it and interrupt as many shipments as you can. Right?"

Doctorow nodded, not quite sure what Bolan was getting at.

"Let's let a shipment through," said Bolan. "And follow it."

"Political consequences could—"

"In this business," said Mack Bolan, "nobody ever did achieve much by worrying about the political consequences."

9

Crate after crate came down the conveyor belt. The belt stopped only to let another cart be pulled into place, then ran again, unloading the cargo hold of the Avianca 747. The wooden crates were marked Coffee, and in fact the air around them smelled of coffee beans. With crates stacked high on each cart in a long string, the operator of an electric tractor would pull his little train away from the 747 and head for a warehouse.

Because the cargo came in from Colombia, it got special attention from the DEA. The country's chief exports were two crops: coffee and cocaine. At the warehouse, customs inspectors were waiting. More conspicuous were the narcs, a dozen of them, three holding dogs on leashes.

Men pointed to crates chosen at random. Warehouse men opened the selected crates, prying off their lids with small crowbars. A German shepherd, straining at its leash, came forward to sniff. Other dogs prowled among the unopened crates, sniffing at the wood.

Mack Bolan and Doc Doctorow stood in the half-dark emptiness of the warehouse, out of sight to all but those who made a special effort to see them.

One man who made that effort came across the floor. "Got one," he said.

Doctorow nodded. "You have your orders. Keep track of it, but keep out of sight."

Bolan checked his watch. It was a little before eleven. The Avianca 747 had come in with the stream of international

traffic that landed on Kennedy Airport in the afternoon. It
had stood at the International Arrivals Building for two
hours, while passengers and crew left and the baggage was
unloaded and hauled to customs. Then, as the gate was
needed for a departing aircraft, it was pulled back by a
tractor, and an Avianca ground crew had taxied it to the
cargo area of the huge airport.

As it was being unloaded of cargo, inspectors and dogs
went over it inside.

The searching delayed the airplane, and the airline protested once more. The DEA was thorough, just the same.
Narcs checked the wheel wells, the fuel tanks, the cockpit,
the rest rooms . . . every inch of the big plane.

It was clean. Except for one cargo crate marked Coffee,
which in fact contained coffee—plus twenty kilos of cocaine.

"We could hit the crate with fluorescent paint," the narc
suggested to Doctorow.

"No," said Bolan gruffly. "They're not dumb. They
might check for that. And if they get a glow with *their* ul-
traviolet lights, that crate becomes an orphan."

The narc glared at Bolan for a moment, obviously wondering where he got the authority to say anything, but the
cold return gaze silenced him. He returned to his work
without even waiting for a confirming word from Doctorow.

They settled down to wait. That crate could sit there for
a week, or it could be picked up in the next ten minutes.

LUISA GOYA TRUDGED wearily up the street toward the
building where Juan Llorente kept his apartment. She had
spent the day walking the streets in the financial district,
dressed like a hooker in skimpy shorts and high heels, her
bristly red hair getting its own share of attention. All day
she'd had to fend off propositions. She wondered how many
would have been made if people had known she was carrying in her handbag the .41 Magnum pistol that had killed a

Chinese professor and a NYPD cop in the park behind the public library on Saturday.

Juan Llorente would be angry with her for going downtown and stalking through the streets looking for the man who was responsible, one way or another, for the death of her husband and children. But the streets of the financial district, where he harassed dealers, was the only place she knew to find him. She prayed for the Blessed Virgin's help to lead the man into her path.

A SMALL BEIGE VAN PULLED into the warehouse, through double doors that had opened to let it in. Bolan and Doctorow watched from the shadows of stacked crates.

A man walked out into the middle of the warehouse and raised an arm. The van stopped. He walked over and spoke to the driver. Then the van went into reverse, backing toward a stack of crates.

Two men left the van and opened the rear door. The man who had told them where to back the van walked over to the stacked crates and pointed at one, two above the bottom. The two men had to unstack crates to get to the one they wanted. In a minute they reached the designated crate and lifted it into the back of the van and closed the doors.

The driver spoke with the warehouse man for a moment and handed him something.

By that time Bolan was already on his way out of the warehouse through another door.

He was riding a bike again. Only this time it was a Honda, a light, maneuverable motorcycle he liked better than the hog he had used that morning. He carried the Beretta in leather under his black nylon jacket. The Desert Eagle and some other weapons were in the locked saddlebags of the motorcycle.

Their routine, his and Doctorow's, was pretty much the same. Doctorow used the same car he'd used earlier. Bolan didn't wear a helmet tonight. He didn't have a radio clamped to his head, but he carried a Handie-Talkie in a leather case.

The van worked its way through the complicated tangle of interior roads of Kennedy Airport. The driver had done this before, obviously. Bolan, following on the nimble bike, had no trouble staying behind him, but Doctorow was already lost.

The van pulled out into the Van Wyck Expressway and accelerated, rushing north into Jamaica, Queens. It was a road Bolan knew well; he had traveled back and forth to the airport on it many times. What he didn't know was Jamaica itself, and when the van left the expressway at Jamaica Avenue and headed east, Bolan was in unfamiliar territory.

The Handie-Talkie squawked. It was Doctorow, pleading to be told where Bolan was.

"I don't know. He took the Van Wyck and turned off at Jamaica Avenue. I'm with him, but I don't know where."

"West on Jamaica?"

"East!"

"Try to get oriented."

"Yeah, sure."

The warrior was glad he was riding the little bike. It was good for this kind of chase. Inconspicuous. Not too loud. Good acceleration.

He followed the van through a neighborhood of stores and bars and gas stations, a good many of them still open. People were on the streets. He knew what they meant when they said the city never slept. New York never did, for sure. Guys were out on these streets. And gals. There seemed to be a lot of laughing and good times on a Monday night as midnight approached.

Now the beige van turned south, into a neighborhood of small, dark houses, where people weren't still up and laughing. Then the van turned again and yet again, and they seemed to be going into an area of light industry.

Warehouses lined the streets, along with some decrepit-looking brick buildings that were, or maybe had been, small factories.

It was the perfect place for a lab. Bolan dropped back. There was little traffic on these streets, and he didn't want to be identified.

The van made a couple more turns, then the brake lights glowed, and it stopped in front of a two-story building of soot-stained brick. Across the street was an auto-salvage yard. Next door was a veterinary clinic making the night wretched with the incessant yapping of caged dogs. The building on the other side was not only vacant; it was collapsing—the roof was down inside it, and every window yawned at the night, without glass. Evidently no one lived within three or four blocks.

The veterinary clinic was lighted. Probably someone was on duty there, sleeping but on duty. Everything else was dark.

Well... it looked that way. Getting closer, it was easy to see that the windows of the dark brick building were painted over.

"Doc?"

"Where are you?"

Bolan read the street markers.

"It'll take me twenty minutes. Cool it till I get there, will you?"

"Sure," Bolan replied.

Doc Doctorow was a good man. But there had been few men Mack Bolan wanted to take on as partners. He'd taken on some very capable men—and he mourned more of them than he wanted to count. Good guys. Great guys. Brave and capable, honest and dedicated—the kind of guys that would make the world work, if it ever would work again. Men who put their lives on the line for what counted.

Doctorow was that kind too, and Mack Bolan did not want to get the man killed.

Bolan would not wait twenty minutes. With any kind of luck, it would be over in twenty minutes.

He stuck the Honda bike alongside the veterinary clinic. Opening the saddlebags, he took out the tools of his trade. Tossing aside the black nylon jacket, he was dressed in a black T-shirt, black pants, black boots. The Beretta hung in its leather, and now he hung the Eagle. He had some other things, too, that he hung on straps on his chest.

The guys in the van carried the crate through the front door of the brick building.

Bolan was glad for the unhappy yapping coming from the veterinary clinic. Their noise covered the sound of other dogs who might have set up a howl at the presence of a stranger in the neighborhood, plus the unavoidable noise caused his movements on pavement scattered with debris and gravel.

He had to do a recon, first behind the building. He found nothing much. There was no alley, just a strip of vacant land covered with weeds and litter. The back door was solid steel and secured with a heavy padlock—there was no telling what kind of lock was inside.

Crossing behind, he came to the abandoned, collapsing building on the other side. He went in, smelling decay and the stench of neglect. Climbing was no great problem. He climbed up the inside of the ruin, part of the way up the inclined wreckage of the roof. Reaching the top, he had an easy jump over a narrow space to the adjoining building, which housed a crack lab.

The roof wasn't so sound, and he was careful crossing it.

He came to the door leading down. It was a flat steel door without any lock outside. He knelt and gently pried the rusty old door up. It wasn't secured from inside. He turned it back, and the inside of the building was open to him.

Below the door was a steel ladder. Bolan waited a minute, staring down into the darkness and letting his eyes adjust, then he descended the ladder to the wooden floor of the building's second story.

He'd been right: it *was* a crack lab. The smell of ether was heavy on the air.

That was one of the ways of making crack. They dissolved cocaine in ethyl ether. The ether evaporated rapidly over heat, leaving behind a brown, crystalline solid—crack. They broke the solid up into small rocks that could be smoked in pipes. The stuff was more powerful and more addictive than pure white cocaine ever was.

If heroin was added to the cocaine before it was poured into the ether, then sotty was the final product. Even stronger, even more addictive than crack.

Bolan took a small flashlight from his pocket and checked out the second floor. This building had once been a warehouse for shoes, and boxes of shoes still stood in dusty stacks. The second floor contained at least a thousand pairs in boxes obscured by black dust.

Bolan located the stairway. No doors blocked the way to the first floor. Looking down the dusty, rickety stairs, he could see light from the rooms below. And he could also hear sounds. It seemed to him that work was in progress.

Deciding that the silent Beretta was the better initial weapon in this situation, he drew it from its leather. Then carefully he made his way down the creaking old stairs.

The first floor seemed to have served in the same capacity as the second, but with an office to the right of the entrance and the stairs.

He quickly got an idea of the layout. Big double doors open to the street, through which he could see the van that was backed up to those doors, then there was the room he took to be an office, behind a single door, and finally another set of double doors, closed. The lab was undoubtedly behind those doors.

The office was in use. He could hear a rapid-fire exchange in Spanish. Bolan frowned. He'd come to destroy a Vietnamese sotty lab, not a Colombian crack lab. But a crack lab seemed to be what he had discovered, and he'd just have to deal with it, anyway.

Abruptly the office door opened. A pair of hard-looking Hispanics stepped out, one of them carrying a suitcase. A third man hung back in the office.

Bolan had no doubt about what was in the suitcase. Crack. The pair had brought a load of Colombian cocaine here from the airport, and they were taking away a supply of crack for tomorrow's street sales.

One man tossed the suitcase into the van, then stood aside and waited for his partner. The second man spoke to him for a moment, then returned to the office inside after closing the front doors behind himself.

With the doors closed, the entrance area was dark. Bolan came right down the stairs. He paused for a moment and heard casual conversation from the office.

He put his ear to the double door for a moment. The people inside, men and women, were speaking Spanish.

He retreated silently to the area under and behind the stairs.

Just in time. The doors to the lab were opened, flooding the entrance with light, affording a glimpse of what was going on in the big room.

It was a crack lab. He'd had no doubt of it, but what he saw confirmed it. They had pried open the crate just delivered, and some of the women were pulling out the coffee, carrying bags of fragrant coffee beans to a long table where they put them down beside handbags and umbrellas. Apparently the women took the coffee home. Men were pulling out plastic bags of the white powder.

The crate had contained about ten bags of cocaine. Bolan guessed each bag contained a kilo—2.2 pounds. If his guess was right, tonight's delivery was worth almost eight million dollars, street value, and something less than twenty-five percent of that, wholesale. The market price of the stuff swung wildly up and down, but it was worth close enough to his estimate.

Tonight's delivery apparently resupplied a lab that had been out of cocaine, since he could see no more bags of powder anywhere. There was a supply of crack waiting to go out—most of it already packaged in vials but some in glass jars, looking like rock candy. The two men from the office came across and into the lab. Now they watched as the bags of cocaine were weighed.

They put each bag on the scale—a butcher's scale, like in a meat market, and marked in kilos instead of pounds. Everyone stared at the pointer, and they wrote the numbers in little notebooks.

The man who had made the delivery stepped up to the scale, waved back a man with a bag of cocaine and put a small steel weight on the scale. The pointer went to one kilogram, exactly. Satisfied, he stepped back and nodded, and the weighing went on.

Only a couple of men in the lab took no part in the weighing. It was easy to see why. They were the guards, each one carrying a submachine gun hanging on a strap.

The submachine guns were Beretta Model 12s, cheap and ugly guns but entirely reliable for chopping up close-range targets. These had 40-round box magazines hanging out of them—awkwardly long but giving the two gunners plenty of ammo for repeated bursts.

The two bosses wore light jackets through which their weapons made visible bulges. Bolan also noticed another weapon lying on a table, a Heckler & Koch MP-5. Somebody here meant business.

That was just fine with the Executioner. He was ready, but something happened before he could make his move.

Suddenly the outside doors were thrown open, and the man from the van ran in, yelling, "*¡Policía! ¡Narc! ¡Narc!*"

The gunners in the lab had no intention of giving in to a cop or a narc. Not with eight or ten million dollars of merchandise at stake. They ran from the lab—the two gunners with Beretta 12s, accompanied by the two bosses. One of the bosses had picked up the H & K MP-5. They carried among them enough firepower to stop a company of soldiers, much less one officer of the DEA. Bolan knew it had to be Doc-

torow outside, and now his job would be more complicated.

He had come to destroy the lab, but before he could, he
had to save one blundering narc.

The two guards and two bosses ran outside so fast they
did not notice the black-clad warrior behind them by the
stairs. He stepped out and followed them, still not noticed.

One of the Beretta 12s stuttered a burst. And the man who
had fired it staggered back and fell, his weapon clattering to
the street.

Doctorow was not defenseless.

Bolan slipped outside and along the brick wall of the front
of the warehouse. The crack makers were so intent on the
blue Ford and the man firing from behind it that they saw
nothing else.

Doctorow was on the far side of the Ford, which was
stopped in the middle of the street. He was crouched behind the hood and had taken out the man who had stitched
the Ford with 9 mm slugs.

The crack makers quickly took cover behind the beige
van. The boss with the H & K levelled it and poured a burst
into the rear of the Ford, apparently hoping to set it on fire.
When he saw his burst had been ineffectual, he began to yell
orders.

Bolan understood the idea—some of them would pin
down the narc with bursts of fire while others crossed the
street and reached a point where they could get a shot at
him.

The boss gave the word. He blasted the Ford with his H
& K, as did another gunman who had picked up the Beretta
that had been dropped and was making a dash for the far
side of the street with a companion.

Bolan dropped the man with the Beretta 12. The crack
makers did not realize that the shot had come from behind
them. Bolan's own Beretta, his 93-R, firing subsonic rounds
and equipped with a flash hider, took out the running man

so quietly they supposed he had been taken by the narc behind the Ford.

The second man dropped to his knees to recover the submachine gun. He never rose. Bolan's shot put him out of running for good. He just flopped over, to the surprise of the men around the van.

The van rocked under the impact of a stream of bullets. Doctorow had a submachine gun, too.

Doctorow was full of surprises.

So was Bolan. The time had come to take out the boss with the H & K. That weapon was dangerous.

He shoved the 93-R into its leather and drew the Desert Eagle. It was also time to let these brutes know they had a second enemy, behind them.

The boss with the H & K was yelling orders when the .44 Magnum slug from the Eagle decapitated him. That gruesome sight was finally enough to make the others run. The battle was over. Two of the fleeing men dropped their weapons as they raced away into the darkness.

Bolan stepped back inside to find the lab deserted. The women had retreated through a back door.

Bolan was ready for the next step. He had come intending to set a fire. He pulled the pin from a thermite grenade and tossed it across the lab toward the cans of ether.

"Hey! Hey! Evidence!" Doctorow yelled as he ran into the building.

Bolan pushed him back, through the outer doors.

The grenade went off with a whoosh, making a white-hot fire. Within a second the cans of ether blew up, and the shipment of cocaine was lost in the roiling fire.

Bolan tossed another thermite grenade into the van. In a few seconds the van was filled with fire. The crack destined for the street the next day burned.

Doctorow was mumbling something about prosecutions.

"A lot of street dealers don't have anything to sell tomorrow," Bolan replied coldly. "And I don't know about you, but I don't want to be here when somebody has to explain who those bodies are. You think you can ride on the *back* of a motorcycle?''

BACK IN DOCTOROW'S OFFICE, they found a message waiting for them.

"You'll be interested in this," Doctorow remarked as he handed Bolan a faxed report from Washington. It was from the FBI and marked secret.

We find no reason to suspect the bona fides of Major Quant Chanh Thang. He was admitted to this country under the program for facilitating the admission of Vietnamese who served the cause of democracy during the war in Vietnam. During his time in this country, he has conducted himself entirely properly and is neither known to have committed any offense against our laws nor is suspected of any such conduct.

You will be aware of course that Major Thang was a dedicated anti-Communist and served the cause of democracy with distinction.

"Guess it would be safe to call him, wouldn't it?" said Bolan. "I remember the man the same way the FBI does."

JUAN LLORENTE WAS NOT asleep, though it was after two in the morning. Luisa Goya was not asleep, either, though for a different reason.

Francisco Pardo and two other men dedicated to *la hombría* sat in the living room, engaged in a grim conference.

Luisa lay in bed in Llorente's bedroom, turning painfully and trying to find enough ease to let her go to sleep. She had been right that Llorente would be angry with her for going downtown looking for the man with the sharpshooters' medals. To put emphasis on his words, he had flogged her with a belt. She had not bled, but the welts were swollen and ugly and sore.

She could hear them talking in the living room.

"The shipment! The whole damned shipment! Plus a lot of crack!"

"It has to be the loner, with maybe one more man. The damned loner—and I suppose the one who leaves the medals around."

"We don't know who the hell he is," said another man. "We don't know what he looks like. How can you deal with somebody when you don't even know what he looks like?"

Juan Llorente glanced toward the bedroom door, where he knew Luisa Goya was sweating and feeling the sting of her whipping. He had her under control now, he was sure. "I know someone who has seen the man," he said. "We can arrange to put her where she can finger him for us."

10

Bolan punched in the number left by Major Quant Chanh Thang. The telephone rang three times, then it was answered.

"Major Thang. Sergeant Mercy here."

"Sergeant! What a pleasure to hear from you! Oh, yes, it is a great pleasure. May I dare hope your situation is such that we can meet?"

"I am always available to a patriot like you, Major," said Bolan. "Always. I remember—"

"Yes," the major interrupted. "We do remember old times. Bad times. Good times. It will be my very great pleasure to have you as my guest for dinner, Sergeant. A glass of wine—"

"The war isn't over, Major," Bolan cut in.

"*My* war is over, Sergeant," said the major. "That is, my chief war. I know you have gone on, fighting again to save civilization. I have—"

"The war is never over, Major," said Bolan. "Not as long as the world is what it is."

"Yes, of course. And in that regard we remain allies. Allied in friendship, in any case. Sergeant…what can I do for you? What can you do for me?"

"You might be able to help me, Major," said Bolan. "Some of the members of the Vietnamese community in New York have become involved in selling a vicious mixture of cocaine and heroin. I'm sure you know."

"I know what I read in the papers, Sergeant. What I see on television and hear on the radio."

"Yes, but maybe you know the names of people I should contact."

"Maybe I do. So, when can we meet? Could it be for dinner Wednesday evening?"

"I'll pass on the dinner myself," Bolan said. "But you could go ahead and I'll just have a drink or two."

"Very well, though you may change your mind once we're there. As I remember, Sergeant, you never acquired a taste for French food. You like steaks and potatoes. So just in case...do you know a restaurant called the Palm, on Second Avenue?"

Bolan knew the place well. On the sidewalk outside the Palm was where he'd rid the world of the vicious Stogie Lentini, during his fight against the corruption of New York construction unions. Lentini, too, had appreciated a good steak—also the sixteen-year-old girl he'd had with him that night. Bunny Kennelly. The girl had been returned to her family after that night.

"I do retain my old habit of eating rather late," said Major Thang. "Would you mind meeting me as late as eight-thirty?"

"That'll be fine," Bolan agreed.

TWO MINUTES LATER the telephone rang in the apartment of Marshal Le Xuan Diem. The marshal's girl, still clad in black leather, answered.

"Thang," she said as she handed the marshal the telephone.

"Good morning, Major. What news?"

"My friend will meet me for dinner at the Palm tomorrow night at eight-thirty."

"Ah. That is good. That is very good."

"I will carry out the terms of our contract, probably when we leave the restaurant. You may, however, want to back me up. My friend is a dangerous man, you know."

"I have every confidence in you," said the marshal. "But you are right. I will provide backup. How do you plan to do the job?"

"With a pocket pistol," said the major. "After a friendly dinner, reminiscing about old times and talking of nothing significant, he should be off guard. He trusts me. I could hear it in his voice."

"Very good," said the marshal.

"When the job is finished, I shall call on you for payment."

"Very good," the marshal replied once more.

When he had put down the telephone, Marshal Diem turned to Pete Nhu and smiled. "The major is having dinner with Bolan at the Palm tomorrow evening at eight-thirty. He plans to kill him as they leave."

"I will be ready," said Nhu. "And we will save half a million dollars."

"Save...?" the marshal asked, frowning.

"I offered you a million to get rid of Bolan," said Nhu. "You hired the major for half of that. Now, as it turns out, the major will set Bolan up for us. Maybe he will succeed in killing him. Maybe he won't. It doesn't make any difference. We will lay down enough fire to kill anyone on the block. Bolan... and the major, of course... I will pay you that half million you would have profited on the transaction, and I will save the other half million."

"Your plan is good except for one thing," said Marshal Diem.

"Which is?"

"I, too, planned on killing Major Thang. Which would have resulted in my having the whole million."

Nhu laughed. "We will not dispute the money, my friend," he said. "I will have to pay off my gunmen. Whatever is left of the million after I do that is yours. Say, three-quarters of a million."

Marshal Diem nodded gravely. He did not say what was in his mind—that Pete Nhu had become too self-important, insufficiently respectful, and sooner or later would have to be dealt with severely.

CAPTAIN FRANCIS O'BRIEN—again in civilian clothes—met with Bolan and Doctorow on a bench in a green park on the East River in lower Manhattan.

"It's infuriating how long things take to come together," said O'Brien. "The red Porsche. It was found abandoned in a parking lot last night. I mean, all day the force had been looking for a red Porsche—the car from which an almost-fatal shot had been fired at a police car—and for God knows how many hours it had been sitting there. The local precinct even checked out a stolen-car report in that parking lot and didn't notice the hottest car in town—and a damned distinctive car at that—sitting there."

"How's the officer who was shot?" Bolan asked.

"Going to lose the sight of one eye," said O'Brien. "Every cop in town would like to get his hands on the man who did that."

"Fingerprints?" asked Doctorow.

"Yeah," said O'Brien. "All over the Porsche. But the only ones that are on record belong to a parking-garage attendant in Chinatown. Whoever the other prints belong to, the guys have never been arrested."

"Registration?"

"Car belongs to an auto-leasing company uptown. Leased to a guy named Chak Drang, which is of course a false name. Paid in advance with traveler's checks. He'd had the car about two weeks."

"A Vietnamese, then," said Bolan.

O'Brien nodded. "An Oriental anyway. He dropped some cash on the lease clerk and was allowed to take the car without putting down a security deposit or really giving much identification. The young woman put false information on the papers to make it look like she'd done the lease legit."

"He was on his way into Brooklyn when he figured out he was being followed," Bolan said.

"He had a cellular phone in the car and called in troops to knock you off his tail."

Bolan looked thoughtful. "Brooklyn... No coincidence. He was running over to stash his money and pick up a new supply of his poison."

"Brooklyn's a big town," said O'Brien.

"We ought to be able to find the man who shot the cop," Bolan asserted grimly. "One way or the other."

BOB LAC DID NOT GET his sotty from Pete Nhu. He had his own factory in Brooklyn, a lot smaller, but still his own factory.

The honored one had not meant for his boys to learn as much as they did. Not to depend on him, for instance. Not to depend on anyone.

Marshal Diem had called and raised hell. How had Bob dared to shoot a cop? What was he trying to do? A *cop,* for God's sake!

The marshal had outlived his usefulness.

So had the honored one. Never again would Bob Lac demean himself before any man as he had demeaned himself, from childhood till young manhood, to that evil old man.

He and Pete should have killed the old man. One of them surely would have done it soon, if the Colombians hadn't. Of course, they still hated the enemy for it.

Independent. That was what he was, at last. Independent.

If Pete Nhu didn't understand that the marshal must go, then Bob Lac would take care of Marshal Diem on his own.

His lab was in Bensonhurst, Brooklyn, in the cellar under a dry cleaner. People parked in front and carried in clothes, and no one in the neighborhood suspected that the clothes carried in sometimes contained plastic bags of cocaine and heroin. Nor was it known that when people picked

up suits or slacks or sweaters, often bags full of crack or
sotty hung inside.

Bringing in the ether was, of course, easy. Dry-cleaning
fluid—who would suspect those contained ether? The exhaust fans from the dry-cleaning shop blew the ether fumes
out into the wind, where they were caught and further dispersed by the outside fan on a big air conditioner. No one
suspected the occasional scent they caught from the lab was
the smell of ether.

Bob Lac's lab was not hidden. It was in plain view, on a
busy street. He laughed at NYPD and the narcs.

He had laughed a little more heartily until yesterday,
when he had been compelled to shoot a NYPD officer. It
wasn't so funny now. That's what Marshal Diem had called
about.

You could take a lot from somebody. To have them point
out a mistake you knew you'd made was too much. Diem's
arrogance was intolerable.

BOLAN STOOD at the corner of Fulton and Adams in
Brooklyn, just outside the subway station, casually survey-
ing borough hall.

Yeah. It was the same thing here. The dealers were more
careful here, a little less conspicuous, but you could identify them if you looked.

A lot of people had the wrong idea about Brooklyn. It
wasn't a slum. For damned sure, it wasn't that. A hell of a
lot of people lived in Brooklyn—more than two million of
them—and they were supplied with the full services a city its
size had. Including the good and legit things, and unfortu-
nately, also the bad, too, including dealers in poisons.

He could do what he had done in Manhattan—hassle the
dealers, destroy their merchandise. He could try to follow
their suppliers back to their wholesalers, their wholesalers
back to the labs.

He had done that, and all it had accomplished so far was a threat from the mayor to call in troops to stop the violence in the streets.

He'd destroyed ten or twelve million dollars' worth of their poison since he started five days ago and cut down some of their guys. More than a few.

Still, could he say he'd made a dent in what they were doing—what the Colombians were doing with their crack and the Vietnamese with their sotty?

He'd just stirred them up, like hornets. What he needed was a hard hit. He needed to know he'd made a difference. He'd invited them to come after him. That was the point, wasn't it? He wanted them to come after him.

Maybe Major Thang could give him the Intel that would make a difference.

LUISA GOYA WALKED a little stiffly. The welts on her back hurt. She sighed as she climbed into a BMW on the street just outside the New York Stock Exchange. She had sweated in the July heat, and her salty sweat stung the welts.

But maybe she deserved the hurt. Her father had brought her up to understand that a man had the right to punish a disobedient woman. Carlos had beaten her for disobedience. Men who lived by the code of *la hombría* thrashed their unruly women. That was understood, and if a woman didn't like it, she didn't give herself to a man who lived by that code.

The man behind the wheel looked at her inquiringly.

"No?"

"No," she said.

She had not seen the sharpshooter on the streets. She had walked through all the blocks of the financial district, looking for the American, but she'd had no luck.

The driver was Francisco Pardo. She was afraid of him, but she knew he was a man who would stop at nothing to avenge their people.

And they had many to avenge.

"GET IN," DOCTOROW SAID.

"No deal," Bolan answered.

"That's right," Doctorow responded. "Standing around on the damned street is no deal. This isn't doing any good, big guy. Let's go. We might as well follow one of them."

"It's a go. Check the little gray Honda. He's been around the block too many times. Either he's a cop, or he's watching the dealers."

"You got 'im."

The Honda—it was silver-gray—moved in a large circle around Brooklyn Borough Hall, covering half a dozen blocks. It didn't carry anything, didn't stop to exchange briefcases, but as Bolan had noticed, the guy in the passenger seat had a tough weapon in his lap.

"Enforcer," Bolan said.

"So we watch," Doctor offered.

"Might see something interesting."

Doctorow was driving a car confiscated under the narcotics law. It was a Lincoln Town Car, a beast of an automobile, long and wide as a barge. It was so powerfully air-conditioned that Bolan was actually cold sitting in the passenger seat.

"Vietnamese," said Doctorow.

Bolan nodded. He had seen that already, that the dealers checked by the silver-gray Honda were Oriental. That meant they were selling sotty.

Shortly the Honda turned south, and in a few minutes it was on the Gowanus Expressway, accelerating rapidly. Following it wasn't a problem. The big Lincoln was surprisingly quick. Being heavy and wide, it was also sure. Doctorow guided it confidently through traffic, keeping well back but not losing his mark.

The Honda kept going south, all the way to the entrance to the big Verrazano-Narrows Bridge. For a moment it looked as if it would proceed over to Staten Island, but then it turned onto the Shore Parkway and headed east.

The Honda followed the Shore Parkway east and south, around Fort Hamilton and along Gravesend Bay. It passed by the exits for Coney Island, where on Sunday Bolan had met Deirdre Levantis. Moving east, the Honda finally exited and turned south into the waterfront community called Brighton Beach.

"This is where Russian émigrés congregate," Doctorow remarked. "On some of these streets you'll hear more Russian than English."

"Refugees from communism," said Bolan.

"Most of 'em, yeah. But like a lot of other émigré communities, a few of them are into organized crime. It's a damned shame, but that's what they do. There are some sordid little rackets working out of Brighton Beach."

"That's the deal sometimes," Bolan commented. "With any group of people, there will be bad apples."

Brighton Beach was no big community, a little beach town at the edge of a huge city.

"Watch this," Doctorow said curtly.

The Honda was pulling over to the curb. A couple of men with wide cheekbones—Russians, most likely—turned abruptly and stared at it.

It was impossible to tell from this distance just what the two Russians thought of the occupants of the Honda. Bolan could see, just the same, that it was no friendly reaction.

In fact, it was totally unfriendly. One of the Russians grabbed a small automatic from his pants pocket.

He was too slow, or maybe he never had a chance, facing a weapon already aimed at his face. He toppled back, dropping the automatic to the sidewalk.

The other Russian threw up his hands, but it didn't make any difference. Within seconds he fell, his body dropping, draped across his companion's.

The weapon had been equipped with a silencer, and people only a little distance away on the street didn't at first realize what had happened. By the time they did, the silver-gray Honda was accelerating smoothly, calmly leaving the scene.

It would take the police a little while to figure it out. Bolan and Doctorow understood it instantly. The two Russians had seen fit to do a little trading themselves. A shopping bag lay on the concrete beside the two bodies, probably containing money and drugs. It looked like a territorial struggle, all right.

"Stay back," Bolan commanded. "They'll be nervous now. Watching out behind. Just stay back. Let's see if we can find out where they go next."

The Honda went north a block, then west, and returned to the Shore Parkway.

This time it did not stay long on the parkway. Before long it turned off and headed north, into Bensonhurst.

BOB LAC SPENT LITTLE TIME in the cellar under the dry-cleaner shop, watching his people churn out the drug for street use. It was the most amazingly profitable operation anyone had ever thought of, but he didn't need to stand around and keep an eye on things. Others usually did that for him.

In the first place, it stank. The ether fumes could give a man a headache. Besides, it was dangerous. The ether fumes turned people sleepy and careless. And ether was not just inflammable; it was explosive.

There was always the possibility that the narcs might find the lab, and it wouldn't be a good idea to be found there. Nevertheless, he stopped by regularly for brief checkups.

He was there when the silver-gray Honda pulled up to the curb outside and two men came in to report.

They seemed hardly to notice him. His subordinate in the dry-cleaning shop was George Giap, and the two gunners reported to Giap, speaking only to him.

That was the way Bob Lac wanted it. It was something more he had learned from the honored one—to establish levels of safety between himself and the street business. Elementary. Anyone knew that. But he had learned it from Vgo Nguyen Minh, the honored one. He marveled sometimes at how innocent he had been when the honored one began his education. He could wish he hadn't learned everything he'd been taught, but most of it had served him well.

He stood apart, behind the counter, listening to the two men report to George Giap. He pretended deference to Giap, as if he worked for George instead of the other way around.

Business had gone well that day. The two gunmen had made their distribution and collections as ordered. Then they had driven to Brighton Beach to see if the Russian encroachers had been on the street. Good fortune had pursued them all day. Two Russians had been dealing on the street. They would deal no more.

The two men handed over a gray suit, which they had carried in on a wire hanger. The jacket was buttoned, and inside, out of sight, hung a plastic bag full of cash.

Giap went to the back of the shop and returned with a yellow sport coat and blue slacks on a hanger. Again, there was a plastic bag inside. The bag contained sotty for the two men to deliver to their dealers.

"Stone killers," Giap remarked to Lac once the two men were outside the shop.

Bob Lac nodded. "I know them," he said. "Even if they're not smart enough to know me."

"They know you," said Giap. "They are smart enough not to acknowledge you unless you want them to."

"Ah. Well...it has been quiet, George. The Colombians haven't moved since they threw that bomb Saturday night. The sharpshooter-medal man has been on their case the past few days. We haven't even had a dealer hit."

"Maybe we've scared them off," suggested George Giap, though the way he said it told Lac he didn't really believe it.

Lac smiled wryly. "No. That's why I want you to call in troops and guard this place better than we've ever done before. When those two report back at the end of the afternoon, have them stay here. I have a premonition of trouble."

George Giap nodded. His men, Ngu and Hao, would be there, but he didn't have to ask if Bob Lac was going to stay or come back later that night. He knew the answer to that question.

"A WORTHWHILE TRIP," Bolan said to Doctorow. "That's the factory, the dry-cleaner shop."

"*One* of them," Doctorow said, and Bolan nodded in agreement.

"So what do we do now?"

"Those two," Bolan said, "might lead us to something else interesting."

The Honda went north out of Bensonhurst, returning to the streets around Brooklyn Borough Hall, where dealers would be looking for a fresh supply of their merchandise.

"That dry-cleaner shop couldn't be the supply for the whole town, you know," said Doctorow.

"It's gonna be like the crack houses," Bolan commented. "A thousand of them. You knock out one, there's 999 left."

"I have an idea that sotty is not like that," said Doctorow. "At least not yet. What we know of the way they distribute the stuff, it looks like there couldn't be more than a few factories. I have it in mind that there's one really big one somewhere. I'd guess the boss man keeps the process close to the vest. We've never seen a vial of the stuff that didn't come from a Vietnamese dealer. I'd guess it's a small organization—and pretty tightly controlled."

"As opposed to the Colombian crack dealers, who—"

"Who fight among themselves," said Doctorow.

"Hold it!" Bolan yelled.

Doctorow hit the brakes and steered the Lincoln to the curb. Half a block ahead of them the silver-gray Honda had

screeched to a stop as a white delivery truck ran a Stop sign
in front of it.

But it wasn't just a traffic incident. The driver of the truck
was pumping shots from a revolver through the windshield
of the Honda. A big, burly man from the passenger side of
the truck cab trotted around the front and rested the barrel
of a Kalashnikov rifle on the truck's left front fender. A
flower-delivery station wagon had also come to a stop, and
it was obvious that what the two men inside had come to
deliver was anything but flowers.

The Vietnamese with the Mini-Uzi fired his first burst into
the station wagon. The stuttering torrent of 9 mm slugs
ripped through the sheet steel of the station wagon's left
door and flung the driver back against his partner.

The thunderous boom of a shotgun blast hurled a tight
swarm of shot at the man with the Kalashnikov. Half the
pattern hit the fender, but that made no difference, since all
that shot glanced off, carrying flakes of paint and chips of
metal into the face of the rifleman. The pellets that had
missed the fender sieved his arms and shoulders. He staggered back, a mass of blood and torn flesh.

The rifleman had managed to get off one quick burst
from the Kalashnikov, shattering the engine of the Honda.

The Vietnamese with the shotgun was wounded, but he
swung the barrel up just the same and blasted away at the
cab of the truck. The swarm punched in the door, leaving a
huge dent, but the pellets did not penetrate the sheet metal.

It scared the man with the pistol. He ducked back.

But 9 mm slugs from the Uzi bored through. The Vietnamese on the passenger side of the Honda put two bursts
through the truck's door. Then he threw open the door of
the Honda and got out.

The man on the passenger side of the station wagon had
pulled himself out from under the bloody body of the driver
and was out on the far side of the station wagon. He was
armed with a Beretta 92—a NATO, and a police weapon—

and knelt to take aim on the Vietnamese when he came around the back of the station wagon.

The Vietnamese didn't come around. He too knelt, then fired a burst at the pavement under the station wagon.

Some of the ricocheting slugs tore through the legs of the man with the Beretta, and he rolled over on the pavement screaming.

The Vietnamese with the Uzi trotted around to the driver's side of the Honda. He pulled open the door and helped the wounded man out.

Bolan and Doctorow watched. There was not much else they could have done—it was all over so fast that they could not have intervened even if they could have decided on a side to take.

"Not wounded bad," said Doctorow. "Damned if I don't think they're gonna get away."

"Who's gonna stop them?" asked Bolan dryly.

The answer was no one. The pedestrians had fled the explosion of gunfire. Traffic was stopped. People huddled on the floors of their cars and trucks, while others crouched behind parked vehicles and in doorways.

The two Vietnamese walked calmly to a stopped car and spoke to the driver. He got out, hands held apart, nodding emphatically to them. They got in and drove off in his car.

"That's a tough pair of guys," said Doctorow. "Let's keep that in mind when we raid the dry-cleaner shop."

"When you going to do that?" asked Bolan.

"As soon as we can organize it," said Doctorow. "It'll have to be a joint effort—NYPD and DEA. Maybe tomorrow night."

"Tomorrow night . . ." Bolan repeated thoughtfully, but said no more.

11

So the plan was to organize for tomorrow night, Bolan thought. By then, the operation would necessarily have been disclosed to fifty or more guys, and possibly the lab would have been hauled out of the dry-cleaner shop, leaving the cops and narcs standing around with their teeth in their mouths.

The Executioner didn't work that way, and tonight he was doing what he did best.

He parked his rented van two blocks away, a little after midnight. In the rear he changed into his black suit and strapped himself into the harness that carried his Beretta 93-R and the Desert Eagle, plus the other weapons he chose carefully for the work at hand.

He had to be careful anywhere in New York. The Vietnamese and Colombians were obviously willing to let fly wild bursts of 9 mm, with little thought of where all those slugs went. The warrior was not. So...no submachine gun. No rocket launcher. Nothing that could deal death to innocent people on the street.

Besides his two pistols and their extra ammo, he carried rope, a Puuko knife, a light. Slung on his harness were half a dozen antipersonnel grenades.

Urban warfare. It was different from fighting in open country. Tougher, if you cared about the people who could get in the way. Easier if you didn't. If you were any kind of civilized man, you fought at a disadvantage.

The dry-cleaner shop was on a packed city street. Luckily nobody lived above the place, but there were some four-family apartment buildings along the street. A little supermarket across the street. A pool hall, still open, in the next block.

As Bolan changed into his rig in the back of the van, he could see out through the windshield. A car stopped on the street in front of the dry-cleaner shop. A man went in and came out. Quick.

Sure. Dry cleaner. Still doing business after midnight.

But the place showed no other sign of life. The ground floor, where they really did do cleaning, was dark and quiet.

Bolan had done a recon. Besides what he'd seen during the day, he'd walked past the place three times during the evening, as well as around the block. He had the place sure in his mind. His recon had told him there was no back way into the shop. He had to hit it from the front.

He walked silently along the sidewalk toward the dry cleaner. He reached the shop and stepped up the one concrete step into the doorway. There was a lock on the door, but nothing much as far as he could see.

He couldn't be sure whether there would be an alarm or just reliance on strong arms. And he didn't have to be. He had come prepared. He pressed a little pliable thermite into the keyhole, pressing hard, pushing the claylike stuff deeper and deeper into the lock.

It took a lot of it.

A match wouldn't light it. He'd come ready for that. He had in his kit a small coil of pure metallic magnesium. He broke off about four inches of it and shoved it into the plastic thermite as far as it would go.

A match would light magnesium, if a flame was held to it long enough.

The magnesium strip burst into white fire, a white-hot little blaze that produced an intense light. He put his body as close to it as he could to hide the light. The heat from burning magnesium would set fire to water, as the joke went, and it had no trouble igniting the substance Bolan had pressed into the lock.

In a moment the lock had melted and the door was on fire.

Bolan beat out the fire.

Now the door could be opened, which could mean that stepping across the threshold could set off an alarm. But Bolan had also reckoned with the possibility that he'd already set off a silent warning of some kind when he'd tampered with the lock.

There was no point in tossing something into the room to see if that set off the alarm. Any sophisticated alarm would ignore a jacket—even if Bolan had been carrying one—thrown through its beam. A good system, a cheap, minimally good system, would distinguish any inanimate object from a living creature.

No. You had to take your chance. If you burned out a lock without a problem, you had to walk in.

Of course, you could encounter something as primitive as a trip gun. Bolan shone his light around the interior of the dry-cleaner shop, especially into the corners to either side of the door. Then he shone the light on the floor. A simple alarm system reacted to a man's weight on the floor.

There was nothing to be seen.

He shoved the door back and stepped inside, noting that he didn't have to deal with a pressure pad waiting to be stepped on. There wasn't any.

It was too easy.

TOO EASY WAS RIGHT. A hidden light-intensifying television camera was focused on the street door of the dry-cleaner shop. Upstairs, Ngu and Hao stared at a screen. Downstairs George Giap and his gunners watched another screen.

"Ain' no goddamn burglar," said one of Giap's gunners.

"Could wish it was," Giap said. He shoved down the button on his intercom system and spoke to the men upstairs. "You see that?"

"Sure do," said Ngu.

"You know what that is?"

"Better than you do, boss," Ngu replied. "You may be seein' him for the first time. Guys like us have seen him before."

"Him?"

"Well, at least seen what he's done. Never saw him before, personally. But if that's who I think it is, we got big trouble!"

"What? In here? With what we got to take him out?"

"Not enough, boss. Nothing could be enough. You want my advice? Out the goddamn windows. Go! Run! Nothing's enough to face up to what we're lookin' at on that goddamn TV screen!"

"Are you crazy?" Giap raged. "I got enough firepower in here to take out the New York Police Department, and you want me to run away from one man in a blacksuit? Forget it! I order you to attack!"

"You not afraid of that guy, hey?"

"Afraid? Hell, yes, I'm afraid! Were you afraid when those guys tried to hit you this afternoon? Damned right I'm afraid. But how many guys and how much hardware does it take to face one guy? *Go,* dammit! Let's *go!"*

THEY KNEW. They had to know he was in here. Unless they had abandoned the place—which he knew wasn't true, since he'd seen a car there less than half an hour ago.

It had to be a trap.

The warrior stared into the darkness. He listened.

Yeah. The old building creaked. Someone was moving upstairs. He couldn't hear footsteps, but a man moving from one room to another, shifting weight from one area to another, generated small creaks and snaps in the joists, especially where they were joined.

From long experience, Mack Bolan was alert to sounds like these.

He heard a creak from below, too. Stairs, he guessed. A man could climb stairs quietly, but treads and risers flexed under his weight, and there wasn't a stairway that didn't yield some small sounds as a man moved up or down.

So they were moving. Coming. And he was lucky to have had a moment's warning.

Luck? No way. A man who depended on his luck was doomed, because luck always ran out. The Executioner had a moment's warning because he had done his soft probe and knew what to expect in this old building, also because he knew what to look for and what to listen for—and what to read into the things he saw and heard. He did not trust to luck. He trusted to his skills and his experience.

He drew the big .44 Mag automatic from its leather, and like a predator moving through the jungle, Bolan vaulted over the counter and crouched behind it, in the deep shadow where the dim light from the street did not penetrate.

Suddenly the floor and the counter erupted in explosions of slugs and splinters. They were firing from the cellar, up through the floor. Pistols, not bursts from anything automatic, but deadly just the same. A bullet blew apart the cash register.

Bolan leaped away, throwing himself headlong into racks of clothes and then against one of the big steel dry-cleaning machines.

The fire from below followed him, blasting out holes in the floor behind him. They knew he was moving, but obviously they didn't know exactly where.

The fire turned tentative. A shot blew through here, then there, as if they didn't know where to shoot and were just trying their luck.

They'd known when he was behind the counter, and they'd known when he threw himself back into the rear of the shop. Only, from down there they couldn't guess exactly where the counter was, or where the clothes racks were, or the dry-cleaning machines. What was saving him was that they were firing into the ceiling from below, using their best guesses about what was above, and so far they hadn't been exactly right.

Bolan threw himself up on top of the closest dry-cleaning machine. That put steel between him and the floor.

From there he blew three .44 Mag slugs through the floor. He could play the game, too.

The firing stopped.

Bolan clung to the top of the machine and peered into the darkness. Yeah, sure. Somewhere inside was a television camera, one of those that picked up an image in low light and used its electronic circuits to amplify it into something visible on the screen. Well, he'd figured there had to be some kind of security system in here. It didn't make sense for a place like this to operate without one.

So he'd been watched by a hidden TV camera from the moment he came through the door. Probably the system was also one of those that set off a beep when there was motion on the screen.

But he knew something else. Their firing had been too close when he was up by the counter. It had turned wilder when he ran back here. So, he was where the camera couldn't see him.

But once he moved, then maybe the guys upstairs could see him, too.

He didn't want them turning on the lights, either. So where was the panel box? In a shop like this, the electric panel box was usually somewhere in sight, on the wall. It was where a guy could grab it open and shut off everything if something went wrong in one of these machines. What was more, likely there was just one panel box. A small shop wasn't likely to have a separate one for the machines.

He looked around. He didn't see it and decided to risk a sweep of his flashlight beam. He spotted it immediately. The box was mounted where there had once been a rear door, now closed permanently with beams nailed over it. He had seen the same thing outside—boards nailed over the door.

It was time to turn off the electricity. He aimed the Desert Eagle and put a big high-velocity slug into the panel box. Sparks flashed. Now it was as dark in the cellar and upstairs as it was in the shop.

Time to give guys something to think about. He pulled a second .44 Magnum clip from a leather pocket on his harness and held it ready. He emptied the clip already in place through the floor.

Someone shrieked. It was impossible to tell if he had yelled in terror or because he was hit.

Bolan shoved the new clip into the Eagle. It was ready to fire again.

He settled himself more firmly atop the big steel drum of the dry-cleaning machine. This was as good a place as any—better than most—from where to fight.

For the moment maybe the initiative had shifted back to the warrior, where it had been when he came through the door.

Their move. And he had no doubt they'd make it.

NGU AND HAO HAD STARTED toward the stairs when they heard the firing downstairs. So they waited. They wouldn't play little-tin-hero games.

Surprise seemed the best bet against such an opponent. And about the only surprise he was going to get was to find a couple of seasoned veterans against him, men who knew their weapons and didn't do the dumb things guys like George Giap and Bob Lac, among others, did.

Hao had his Mini-Uzi in hand. Ngu's weapon wasn't the short-barreled shotgun he'd used this afternoon. That was what he'd kept in the Honda, for certain uses. His weapon was special, something he'd wanted for years and found not long ago.

The fact was, Ngu was left-handed. Every automatic pistol was awkward for him—every one, that is, until he'd found this .45-caliber Randall, a stainless-steel version of the Colt .45 but *reversed,* designed to be fired by a left-handed shooter. It ejected its empty brass out the left side. The safety and magazine release were on the right. It was made for Ngu, and he appreciated it.

What was more, he was good with it.

Each of them wore an ankle holster with a Colt Commando in the leather.

The two men had worked as a team for many years. They would work that way now.

One reason was that there was no other way out.

THEIR MOVE. The warrior waited, sprawled over the top of the big machine, figuring that wasn't the first place they'd look for him.

He knew they were upstairs and down, and one of them had to move first.

It was the guys downstairs who moved first.

They opened their attack by firing up through the floor again. The slugs came up in a pattern this time, coordinated firing by three or four men, each assigned part of the basement ceiling.

Some of the shots went up through the ceiling above the dry-cleaner shop, and others spanged off the machines, but the steel protected him.

Now he would play on their nerves. He chose to keep quiet and wait, letting them wonder if they had got him.

After a cautious pause, they went through the same routine again. Shots blasted up through the floor, showering the room with splinters and filling the air with dust from falling plaster. The already-shattered cash register jumped off the counter. Clothes whipped back and forth on the racks, shot through with holes.

Silence followed once more.

Bolan heard the stairs creak again—more than a little, announcing two men or more.

There were two doors. Obviously one opened on the stairs to the cellar, one on the stairs to the second floor. Bolan glanced back and forth between them, straining in the gloom to see the first suggestion that one of them was opening.

The worst scenario was if they were able to coordinate their movements. Could both fly open at the same time and fill the whole shop with a storm of fire? They had no electricity, but maybe they had phones, which didn't rely on the main electrical system.

GEORGE GIAP WAS READY to throw open the cellar door, dive to the floor inside the shop and open fire with a Beretta 92, which he would empty and reload and do it again. He had two gunners behind him. They would do the same, one with a revolver that didn't fire as fast but fired accurately in that man's hands.

He believed that Ngu and Hao would be waiting behind the other door and would join in the attack. That much concentrated fire would take care of things. The guy who dropped sharpshooters' medals might be some kind of soldier, even some kind of ghost, but he would not survive all that.

Giap was so confident that Ngu and Hao would understand as soon as they heard the firing that he had no need to grope his way back to the telephone in the darkened cellar. There was no need to call.

The truth was, George Giap was scared. He'd sat here for months, with enough firepower in the place to resist anything, and in a few minutes this one man he had seen as a shadow on the television screen had turned everything upside down.

Instead of taking him out easy, they had to fight him. That was what Ngu and Hao had said . . . that you had to fight this guy with everything you had.

Hard and tough.

BOLAN SAW one of the doors open. A man ducked into the room and let fly a hail of shots without much effort to aim.

He damned near hit Bolan, just the same.

The Desert Eagle spoke for the Executioner. The whole interior of the dry-cleaner shop was lighted in the glare of the muzzle-flash from the big .44 Magnum automatic.

George Giap, his upper body cut open, flew back down the cellar steps, knocking his gunners over backward.

Bolan jerked an MU-50-G grenade off his harness, pulled the pin and tossed it into the open door. The eruption of high-velocity steel shot in the cellar ended the assault from that quarter.

Now he was ready for the assault from the second floor.

NGU AND HAO *DID* HAVE an option, and that was to go out the window upstairs. And they decided to do just that.

They had heard enough to know what had happened below.

Two of them against . . . *him?* No way. They knew better. Anyway, the shooting had produced an emergency call, and they could hear the sirens coming. What might have been a fight between them and the sharpshooter downstairs would soon be a mess—a big police action.

Better to be away. He who fights and runs away lives to fight another day.

BOLAN STEPPED to the cellar door and tossed two more grenades. They would puncture cans of ether, if that was what was down there, and he was quite certain he got it right.

When the cans beneath burst, the volatile chemical erupted in roaring, smoky flame, and the Executioner threw himself through the door and onto the street just before the flames filled the building.

NGO AND HAO TOOK a frightened girl with them as they dropped from a second-floor window to a rooftop behind. From there they clambered down into the alley behind.

Looking back, they saw the whole dry-cleaner shop and the apartment above fill with fire.

Making sotty was a hazardous business.

PETE NHU SAT over a late dinner with Mia. She didn't cook, so they ordered an elaborate dinner from a Chinese restaurant. It had been delivered, and they sat at a candlelit table, surrounded by dishes tempting them with far more food than they could eat—varities of beef, pork, and chicken, plus shrimp and lobster, with vegetables in savory sauces, all to be served over heaps of steamed white rice.

Mia rose from her seat at the table and poured wine for the man she called Bui Dang Nhu because she disliked the American name Pete, which to her ear sounded blunt and crude.

Mia's features were delicate, and her complexion was golden. But she was a child, with a slight frame, and slender like a flower. Despite her youth and air of delicacy, she had, in spite of anything her father and Nhu could do to her, a confident dignity.

Nor was her poise ruffled when the telephone rang and Nhu announced that Bob Lac was on his way up and would join them over dinner. Actually she preferred to have somebody else around because Nhu was less demanding of her.

When Bob Lac rushed in, upset and angry, Nhu tried to wave him over to the table.

"Sit down," he said. "Join us for dinner. Some wine—"

"Whiskey," said Lac hoarsely. He glanced at the girl. He could not ignore her, but neither could he give her a lot of attention. She was Nhu's.

"My lab . . ." he whispered.

"Raided?" asked Nhu.

"I could wish," Lac complained. "Nothing so easy."

"Gone?"

"Gone. Burned out. Everything lost. Giap. Three other men."

"Ngu and Hao?"

Bob Lac shrugged.

"The sharpshooter?"

Lac nodded. "Apparently. Who else? Five good men, with heavy weapons."

"Bolan," said Nhu. "Sergeant Bolan. You've heard the name?"

"I've heard the name."

Mia had heard the name, too. She had heard her father's stories of how things were back home, in the violent years, and she had heard the name of this man Bolan, a hero who had given much of himself in the cause of justice. She kept her expression bland and secretive, but she listened more alertly.

"Come in with me," said Nhu to Lac. "You've never been away from me, really. Like any man, you wanted independence. I won't deny you independence. But for the time being, we must unite against this menace. Come back to me, as it was in the first days with the honored one. When we have eliminated this menace, we will see what new arrangements can be made."

Lac lifted his chin high. "I will never again have, with any man, the kind of relationship I had with the honored one," he said bitterly.

"Nor will I," Nhu replied. "Nor will I ask any man to have such a relationship with me. He is gone, and it's for the best. But we face annihilation at the hands of this man. Come back to me until we eliminate that threat."

Nhu had poured wine for Lac, and, at Nhu's signal, Mia had filled a plate for him with every delicacy on the table. They put these things before the agonized man. He hesitated, then sipped wine and began to sample the food.

"Tomorrow night," said Nhu. "Tomorrow night may bring an end to our troubles. *May?* It must. Tomorrow night

Mr. Bolan will go to dinner with Major Thang at Palm, and—''

"No," said Lac.

"What do you mean, no?"

"The man is a devil," Lac asserted. "I had five good men—''

"Not good enough," said Nhu. He reached across the table and patted Lac's shoulder. "But tomorrow night the devil will at long last meet his match."

"He—''

"If not at the hands of Major Thang," said Nhu, "then at the hands of some other good men. No problem. On the street. A close-range shot in the back. If he is devil enough to escape that, then a tornado of gunfire from half a dozen men."

"Half a dozen is not enough," said Lac. "You don't know—''

"If your men Ngu and Hao show up alive, we will add them to the team," said Nhu. "Bolan is meeting an old friend tomorrow night. He will relax. He won't be suspicious of his old friend. And even Thang doesn't know that we will be waiting outside."

Mia sipped thoughtfully, the tiny frown on her sweet face not revealing her thoughts. They were going to kill...*Bolan?*

12

The sharpshooter would return to Wall Street, of that, Juan Llorente and Francisco Pardo were certain. The trade was there, the contested turf, as well as the money, in the hands of the urbane young men and women of the banks, brokerages and law firms.

Someone had told Llorente that at one time stocks and bonds were sold on a market called the Curb—the tradition being that traders had actually worked on the streets. Well, those traders hadn't made as much money as crack dealers were making on the curbs of the financial district. Some of the fancy-dressed kids who came out of the office buildings were real wheeler-dealers, shuffling billions of dollars around from one company to another. They were the real action in New York.

If the damned Viets hadn't come along with their damned sotty, and in their wake, the sharpshooter...

It was the Viets who'd attracted him to the city—with their viciousness. They were responsible for this trouble.

They'd have to pay. People were going to have to put their differences aside for a while and rid the city of the Viet dealers. It would have to be war—nothing less. And they'd find out who was boss on the streets of New York. There were ten Colombians for every Vietnamese. When it came to war, they didn't have a chance.

But first things first. The sharpshooter had to be disposed of, and here they had an unexpected advantage. Luisa would recognize him.

She had been walking the streets, looking for him, and this morning a cop had hassled her. He took her for what she looked like and gave her a hard time for a while. It was a damned good thing she hadn't been carrying a pistol in her handbag, the way she'd done Monday, and maybe she understood now why he'd given her a good strapping Monday night. But the cop was as stupid as she was. He hassled what he thought was a hooker and never suspected she was the woman wanted for the notorious killings in Bryant Park.

Juan Llorente turned to Francisco Pardo, who sat behind the wheel of their comfortable, air-conditioned BMW. "I'm going to take a break and get myself some lunch," he said. "Listen to me. If she spots the guy, you *follow*. Get me? Don't try to take him out. It won't be so easy. Find out where he goes. We'll get troops together and take him out for sure. Some safe way. Maybe a long shot with a rifle."

Pardo snapped his fingers and said, "Just like that!"

Llorente opened the door and left the car. As he walked past Luisa Goya on the sidewalk, he pretended he didn't know her.

LLORENTE AND PARDO WERE right when they supposed that Bolan would return to the financial district.

It was where the action was, or the best of it, anyway. Since he'd knocked out the Bensonhurst lab last night, he figured that a dealer on the streets had to be supplied from some other factory—which might be the main one he was sure had to exist somewhere.

He was letting Doctorow and O'Brien have their way about the setup. Both of them were irritated about last night. While they were meeting and planning a coordinated raid on the Bensonhurst dry-cleaner shop, Bolan had moved in alone and smashed it.

So as he walked around looking at dealers, watching for a supplier, he was observed by Doctorow and two other narcs, along with two NYPD detectives. If he saw what he was looking for, they would take his signal and put a systematized tail on the supplier. It would be accomplished with cars and radios, with all the paraphernalia of professional police work.

He walked west to the World Trade Center, the pair of towers that were the tallest buildings in New York. Then he proceeded down Broadway to Wall Street.

Nearly every block had a dealer, and most of them had a bonecrusher standing by—a wiseguy, probably armed. The dealers were Vietnamese. They owned this turf. But some of the bonecrushers were just nondescript toughs, hired muscle. That made it more difficult to identify them than the dealers.

On Water Street he saw something strange. A Vietnamese dealer was working the block, backed by two men, not just one. And half a block away, on the other side of the street, an Hispanic dealer was hustling. The Hispanic, almost certainly a Colombian, had his own bonecrushers, maybe two, maybe three; it was impossible to say.

The Hispanic was muscling in on the Viet's turf. Two of his wiseguys walked back and forth, glowering, conspicuously daring anyone to make an unfriendly move.

Bolan turned and glanced at O'Brien's two detectives. They were a couple of shaggy-bearded characters, looking rumpled and down-and-out. One of them caught Bolan's glance and shrugged. Finding a Colombian and a Vietnamese working the same block was not just odd; it was a sign of trouble.

And the trouble came—quick and deadly.

One of the Hispanic wiseguys suddenly stopped swaggering and glowering. He looked shocked. He clutched his chest. His knees buckled, and he sprawled to the sidewalk. He'd been taken out by a high-powered rifle, one with a silencer and modified to cycle subsonic ammo.

Bolan swiftly swept the surrounding area with his eyes. He couldn't spot the rifleman.

Neither could the second wiseguy, but he ran. He couldn't outrun the slug that slammed into his back, and he fell in the gutter.

The dealer stood slack, his head down, his eyes closed, waiting for the shot that would kill him. Stunned, he couldn't move—and knew it wouldn't do him any good if he did.

Bolan still couldn't spot the rifleman. Neither could the two NYPD detectives. They stood staring around, searching windows above the street.

Pedestrians who had at first screamed and run now began to gather around the two bodies. The customers of a coffee shop erupted onto the street. People came out of office buildings. In a minute a crowd had formed.

Sensing that maybe there was safety for him in pressing into the crowd, the dealer abandoned his shopping bag of merchandise and money and shouldered his way into the knot of people gathered around the man who had been shot in the back.

Just then Bolan spotted the rifleman. He was on the roof of the three-story building that housed the coffee shop, behind a sign advertising Marlboro cigarettes. He'd had easy shots, and he was making an easy escape, walking away almost casually across the roof. He'd abandoned the rifle.

Bolan figured there'd be twenty cops on the scene in a few minutes, and one of them might take it in his head to ask the tall man who he was and if that was by any chance a pistol under his jacket. It wasn't a good place to hang around.

He turned and left the block. He saw that the detectives were doing the same. There was nothing any of them could do for the dealers and his wiseguys, even if they wanted to. Besides, the two detectives had their strict orders—not to interfere in anything they saw but to follow Mike Belasko and tail the supplier when Belasko found the one he wanted tailed.

Someone screamed.

Bolan swung around instinctively. The dealer was staggering toward the gutter, a knife sticking out of his back. The crowd scattered a lot more quickly than it had gathered. When the dealer dropped facedown in the street, he was alone; there was no one within fifty feet of him.

LUISA GOYA HAD BEEN in the next block when the Colombian dealer and his bonecrushers were hit. She'd heard the screams.

Suddenly Pardo was beside her. "Move!" he grunted. "Out of this street."

She nodded and strode away quickly.

Luisa was thirsty. She had walked the dusty streets in the bright sunlight for more than two hours, and she wanted something to drink. She looked around for a vendor's cart and saw a bright umbrella a block away on Pearl Street.

She was sweating in the heat. The white shorts were damp, and they were too tight and chafed her skin as she walked. Besides, her high-heeled shoes were not meant for walking a lot, and the calves of her legs had begun to cramp. The fact was, Luisa was thoroughly miserable.

She turned around and looked back toward the crowd and saw the first police car arriving, its lights flashing. Other sirens were screaming in the distance.

The police made her remember that she was maybe the most-wanted criminal in New York. Both Pardo and Llorente had frightened her with stories of what the police would do to someone who'd killed an officer.

Luisa shuddered, as if with a chill. She turned and walked on into Pearl Street, putting distance between her and all those policemen, but became aware of a man behind her, heading in the same direction on her side of the street. Cautiously she turned and glanced back over her shoulder.

The man! It was the man they were looking for! She looked around for Pardo. He was nowhere in sight! Damn him!

Would the man remember her from Saturday night at Casino Bolivar? She'd tried to shoot him. He'd thrown a shotgun in her face and bloodied her nose.

He was walking faster than she was, catching up with her. Maybe he'd already recognized her!

She couldn't run. She'd seen what he could do. He was big and as tough a man as she'd ever seen. Luisa was terrified. She didn't even have a knife in her handbag, much less a gun.

He was coming closer. She could hear his footsteps only a few feet behind her.

Luisa faked a cough. She coughed and reached into her bag and pulled out a handkerchief. As the man passed on her right, she turned away from him and coughed into the handkerchief.

He glanced at her, but only for an instant. He didn't pay any attention to her and didn't seem to recognize her.

She looked all around, hoping that Pardo would show up. Then she saw the BMW, slowly cruising toward her with infuriating casualness.

She didn't dare wave her arms. She raised her chin high and stood unnaturally stiff and erect. Apparently Pardo caught the body language. He accelerated and pulled up beside her.

Luisa jerked the door open. "That's him!" she hissed, nodding toward the tall man striding toward the end of the block.

"Are you certain?"

"*Yes!*"

Pardo picked a microphone off a hook under the dashboard. He pushed the transmit button and said, "Walking north on Pearl. East side. Light blue sport coat, khaki slacks. I'll keep contact till somebody else picks him up."

Luisa settled into the seat of the air-conditioned car. "I found him for you," she said. "Now you get me that fake passport and let me go home."

The thin voice of the radio spoke: "Got 'im. This is Jésus. Contact."

"Keep with him two blocks," said Pardo. "Then somebody else pick him up."

DOC DOCTOROW TIPPED a can of Pepsi and took a big swallow. Bolan, standing beside him, followed suit.

"Simple enough," Bolan said. "Most of them haven't run out of merchandise yet. The suppliers will come."

"Well, we're ready," said Doctorow, and Bolan knew he was right, though they weren't conspicuous. Bolan was not sure even he knew how many of the men and women on the sidewalks were narcs and undercover cops, and which cars and vans in the streets were DEA or NYPD.

He finished his Pepsi and a bag of chips and set off again. In a little while he felt he had his mark.

This supplier meant to be low-profile. He sat in the back seat of a five-year-old black Oldsmobile, a family car. Besides the driver, there was another man in the front. The driver was not Oriental, but the supplier and the other men were definitely Vietnamese. The driver wore a white knit shirt. The two Vietnamese wore suits and straw hats.

The Oldsmobile pulled to the curb beside a Vietnamese dealer. The exchange was made quickly, quietly, then the Oldsmobile moved on.

Bolan nodded to give the signal.

Doctorow was driving one of the chase cars. It was the big Lincoln again. He picked up Bolan, and they followed the Oldsmobile, staying well back.

"Onto Broadway," said Doctorow. "Working slow. He's got more exchanges to make."

The radio crackled. "Got 'im. You can drop off, Doc."

From that point, Bolan knew where the Oldsmobile was only vaguely, listening to street names on the radio.

"Church. Unit two has him."

"Cortlandt. You can drop back, two. New York's finest have him."

"Hey, Doc. Suggest you take Broadway north, in right lane, slow. I think he's coming and will pass you."

"Hello, town hall. H'lo, mayor. 'Bye, Broadway, he's going right! Check that! Where the hell—"

"That driver knows the town. But I got him. This is two. He's going uptown."

"Doc here. I got him again, too. I'm guessing he's going into Chinatown. Which would kinda figure, wouldn't it?"

"I know what's going on," said Bolan. "The car that makes the exchanges with the dealers never goes home to headquarters. It links up in some manner with another vehicle, and they're going to change cars. We've got to watch for the guys in straw hats. They're going to leave that car somewhere . . . and be picked up by another one."

"Makes sense," said Doctorow. He reported it to the other cars. "Watch out for a switch. Let's cover him with two units now."

The Oldsmobile had entered the small neighborhood of Chinatown, where all the signs on shops were in Chinese characters, some in Japanese or Korean characters. Most of the people on the streets were Orientals.

Doctorow gestured at the street and turned to Bolan. "Like any populous neighborhood, this place has its share of crime. It's infested with Chinese gangs. They fight each other. They leave corpses around."

You could almost see it. Elderly Chinese shuffled along the sidewalks, courteously receiving and returning bows and soft greetings. But there were some young ones who boldly shouldered the elderly aside. They swaggered along the streets in black slacks and white vest undershirts, and their pockets bulged with what had to be pistols.

The black Oldsmobile had come to a stop before a Chinese restaurant on Bayard Street. The two Vietnamese got out of the car and, carrying just one briefcase, walked into the restaurant. The driver waved and drove away.

"Couldn't be the headquarters," Doctorow remarked.

Bolan shot him a telling glance. "It isn't. It's their rendezvous point. They transferred all the cash into that one briefcase, and the driver has gone off with empties. A wholesaler will come along in a little while, take that cash and hand over to them another car with some filled briefcases."

"So all we have to do is keep our eyes peeled."

Bolan nodded. "The key is not those two guys. The key is the briefcase. Whoever gets *that* goes to headquarters."

"It can happen inside," said Doctorow.

"Right. I think we've got to go in and hang around."

They were lucky and managed to park the car quickly. The Chinese restaurant was a cool and peaceful haven in a hot, noisy city. Bolan and Doctorow looked around. The two Vietnamese men had taken a table and were sitting looking at the menu. The briefcase was on the floor beside them.

"Lunch for two, gentlemen?"

Bolan nodded at the attractive young woman who had asked, and he followed her to a table. He and Doctorow sat down where they could keep their quarry in sight.

Bolan knew something about Chinese food and ordered an assortment of dishes. Tea had already arrived at their table, accompanied by little cups without handles. The two Vietnamese studied and discussed the menu, both between themselves and with their waiter, and finally decided on an elaborate meal, with wine.

"We may be in here half the afternoon," Bolan said to Doctorow.

"Unless someone comes in and picks up the briefcase while they eat."

"If that happens, I follow the briefcase. Your guys outside stay with me. You stay in here, pay the bill and watch our two friends."

"Got it," Doctorow affirmed.

As soon as food was put before the two Vietnamese men, they stopped talking and devoted themselves to eating. They refreshed themselves with wine, then tea, and ate their way unhurriedly through the elaborate meal while Bolan and Doctorow were eating their simple lunch.

As a dessert of fruit was put on their table, one of the Vietnamese got up and went to the pay telephone in the lobby of the restaurant. He made a short call, then came back.

"Guess what that was about," said Doctorow.

"Calling his contact."

"I'd make book on it. I'm going to pay the check. That pair might make a quick exit."

Doctorow paid for their lunch, but they kept sipping their tea and looked at the fortune cookies that had been delivered to their table along with the bill.

When the Vietnamese were ready to move, they moved fast. One of them summoned the waiter, handed him a credit card, and the two stood up and went to the cash register to sign the credit-card slip.

The older of the two men carried the briefcase.

Bolan and Doctorow stepped out into the sunlight, quickly checking the street.

"Check the Nissan," said Bolan, nodding toward a bright red sports car parked half a block away.

The Vietnamese came out onto the sidewalk. The Nissan shot forward and came to a stop. The older man handed the briefcase to the driver, and the Nissan roared away.

The DEA-NYPD team had been ready for just that. The big Lincoln rushed up to pick up Bolan and Doctorow. It was driven by another narc, a young woman, native New Yorker who knew the streets of the city.

She threw the transmission into Park and leaned over to shove open the passenger-side door. Bolan flung it open while Doctorow grabbed the handle of the back door.

A burst of gunfire shattered the right window and the windshield of the Lincoln.

The young woman had leaned over to reach for the door handle and was almost prone on the seat. That saved her.

She was not hit, except by a shower of glass. Bolan had been standing on a high curb and had bent over to duck into the front seat of the car, so he was unscathed. Only Doctorow was hit with a ricocheting slug just under his arm, a shallow flesh wound.

A second burst of fire followed immediately. The bullets punched into the door, but behind the sheet steel the door was full of other steel—besides the frame, the electric window mechanism, the electric lock components, an air-conditioning duct . . . Only two slugs got through, and they tore into the back of the seat.

The young woman dragged herself back under the wheel, shoved the transmission into gear, and floored the accelerator. The Lincoln glanced off the left rear fender of a BMW and shot into the street, tires shrieking.

In the BMW, Francisco Pardo floored *his* accelerator. But the left rear wheel of the car couldn't turn; the fender was jammed into the tire. The right wheel spun, the car staggered around and then the tire exploded.

Furious, Pardo jumped out, steadied himself against the car for better aim and squeezed off two shots from a Colt .45. His slugs broke through the sheet metal of the rear of the Lincoln and stopped at the wheel of the spare tire.

Pardo took aim again, but before he could get off another shot, he was slammed to the ground by a swarm of buckshot from an NYPD riot gun.

A Chevrolet roared out of an intersection. The driver whipped the wheel around, and the Chevy skidded sideways into the right side of the Lincoln.

A man in the back seat loosed a burst of automatic fire through the windows of the big car. The skid and the impact with the Lincoln had knocked his muzzle skyward, and the slugs tore into the roof.

Bolan had the Desert Eagle in hand now. He took out the gunner in the back seat of the Chevy with a shot that decapitated him. Then he eliminated the driver.

A Ford came up on the left. Doctorow fired through its windshield with his Beretta, but the Ford kept coming. Bolan leaned past him and fired a .44 Magnum bullet into the engine. The Ford shook under the impact. Then its engine locked and blew up.

"Which way, boss?" asked the young woman behind the wheel.

Bolan took stock of their situation with a quick look. "We're not going far in this wreck," he said.

The Lincoln had just about had it. At least two of its tires were shot through. A front fender was jammed in so it could be steered only to the left. It wasn't going much farther.

"Just stop," he said.

"It's over anyway," muttered Doctorow, who was now clutching his bleeding wound.

Another slug snapped through the rear window.

"Get down," Bolan said to their driver. "Stop and get down on the floor."

She pushed down the parking brake, and the Lincoln shuddered to a stop.

On the street, there was a firefight between the NYPD-DEA team and as many as a dozen Colombian gunners who had not yet given up their assignment to kill Colonel Phoenix. As Bolan rolled out of the Lincoln and onto the street, some of the fire shifted to him.

The gunmen in the Ford weren't hurt. They were down beside their car. They in particular still focused their attention on the Lincoln and on the big man who had just rolled out. He was their target. He was what all this was about.

One of them swung the muzzle of an Uzi and sprayed the pavement and the fenders and wheels of the Lincoln.

Men like him were deadly dangerous at close range and not so dangerous beyond fifty feet. A short-barreled automatic weapon is not a target gun. A man who has not practiced with one has a hard time even firing anything close to a tight pattern, much less putting his pattern where he wants it. Besides, few men like him could keep their calm in hard situations. Wiseguys had the stomach to kill but not the guts for combat.

Or maybe he knew he was facing the Executioner.

Bolan swung the muzzle of the Eagle toward the guy. But he didn't get off a shot, because the Colombian suddenly dropped his Uzi, clutched his stomach and fell to his knees.

Bolan looked up. Their driver held a Browning automatic braced on the frame of the shattered driver's-side window of the Lincoln. She had put a slug into the gunman with the Uzi.

"Nice..." he grunted.

"Natalie's the name," she said.

"Watch it," Bolan said.

She nodded at the Ford and fired another shot.

Her slug spanged off the pavement and unnerved another gunman, this one setting himself to get off a shot at the warrior with a long-barreled revolver. Bolan used the two seconds she had given him to drop the gunman.

Twenty blue-and-white NYPD cars had converged on the scene. Officers were closing the streets, herding back the curious. The whole neighborhood was alight with red and blue flashes.

The firing was trailing off as the surviving Colombians looked for ways to retreat.

Bolan was still on the alert for gunmen with ideas.

"Hey—" Natalie pointed at the Desert Eagle "—you got a license for that cannon? In about two minutes, some cops are gonna ask."

Doctorow spoke up a little weakly from the back seat. "No, he doesn't."

"Then you better let me have it for the while," she said to Bolan.

Reluctantly, but sure she was right, Bolan handed her the Desert Eagle. Also the Beretta 93-R. She was a nicely rounded dark-haired woman with a New York accent, pretty in a distinctive way. She handled his weapons all over, putting her fingerprints on them. Street smart.

And she *had* been right. Two cars screeched up, and four officers jumped out, service revolvers ready.

"Federal officers," Natalie said firmly. She nodded toward Doctorow. "One wounded."

One of the officers wore sergeant's stripes. "You the narcs?" he asked.

"Some of them," she said. She shoved her identification case toward him. "We need medics. Also, where's Captain O'Brien?"

Nobody even asked who Mack Bolan was. They took him for a narc. In a minute the medic team rolled up, and two minutes later they confirmed that Doctorow's wound was minor.

When O'Brien rolled around, he went up to Bolan right away. "I've got somebody I want you to look at. Two somebodies, in fact."

A bandaged Doctorow and Natalie went with O'Brien and Bolan in a police car, back to the Chinese restaurant.

A policewomen summoned Luisa Goya out of the back of a squadwagon and marched her toward the captain. Luisa's hands were cuffed behind her back, and she gleamed with sweat.

"Ever see her before?" asked O'Brien.

"Twice. Once at Casino Bolivar…and once on the street this morning."

O'Brien nodded. "Guess what. She's the woman who killed the cop in Bryant Park. Plus the Chinese professor. She knows we've got her dead on those two murders, so she's singing like a canary. Look at the guy over there. You ever see him before?"

Bolan turned and looked at a heavy Colombian man who had been pulled out of the back of a blue-and-white. He was also handcuffed. Bolan shook his head. He'd never seen the man.

"Juan Llorente," said O'Brien. "Kingpin Colombian. And he's in big trouble. He's the one who ordered this war—to get *you*, Belasko, or whoever you are. So Luisa tells us. She thinks we'll take it a little easier on her maybe if she talks. So she's made a big point that she doesn't want to see a lawyer—she just wants to bare her soul.''

"So what's in her soul?"

"She was ordered to cozy up to you and get acquainted Saturday night. Since then, she's been looking for you. For them. This morning she saw you and fingered you. She was with a guy called Pardo, a stone killer. He got his during the battle. Llorente didn't. He's gonna get his one day at a time, at Attica.''

"A good day's work," Doctorow summed up.

"Not so good," Bolan said. "Where's the briefcase?"

13

Mack Bolan had saved Wednesday evening for his get-together with Major Quant Chanh Thang. The major, had picked up distinctly European habits and liked to dine late, so the appointment was for eight-thirty at the Palm, a restaurant supposed to serve the best steaks in town.

"We don't trust your old friend Major Thang entirely," Doc Doctorow said as Bolan shaved in the bathroom of his hotel room.

"I don't trust anybody entirely," Bolan replied. "But Thang was a fighter for his people's freedom, and he was admitted to this country under a special program to let people who risked their lives for us come here and live. If I can't trust him, who can I trust?"

"You'll go armed just the same, I suppose," said Doctorow cynically.

Bolan, his face still half-covered with shaving soap, turned toward Doctorow, who was sitting on the hotel-room bed, and shook his head. "Man," he said. "I go armed *everywhere*. It's in the nature of the business."

"There will be two or three DEA agents around."

"Not you," Bolan countered. "Even if you feel up to it—"

"Natalie," said Doctorow. "And a couple other guys. Don't sweat it. They'll be around, just in case."

"Natalie... I'd just as soon... Hey, Doc! No Natalie, huh? I sometimes get to feeling like I'm bad luck for women."

Doctorow shrugged. "Okay. If I can reach her, I'll call her off."

Bolan came out of the bathroom. He had showered just before he shaved, and he was wearing nothing but a pair of slingshot underpants. Doctorow looked up and could not conceal his awe. The big guy was big. Actually he wasn't that much bigger than the average man; he was maybe six-two, six-three. But he was all muscle, all hard muscle, and his body was marked with scars. None of them disfiguring, none from a wound that would impede his movements—just scars, each one representing a sacrifice made, a pain suffered, in the man's unending war for the things he thought were right.

The warrior figured he'd have to wear a necktie for the occasion, so he pulled on a white shirt, buttoned the collar and tied the tie, then pulled on gray slacks and a navy blue blazer with brass buttons.

The blazer had been specially tailored to cover a shoulder holster and the Beretta 93-R.

For a backup weapon, he carried a Heckler & Koch P7, a compact, concealable 9 mm automatic holstered on his right hip. He liked the P7. He'd never seen another pistol quite like it. It was cocked by squeezing the grip, then fired when the trigger was pulled. If the squeeze on the grip was released, then pulling the trigger wouldn't fire the weapon. It was as safe a pistol as he'd ever seen. A crook had grabbed one out of the hand of a New Jersey state trooper but couldn't kill the officer with it because he couldn't figure out how to fire it. The officer had recovered the pistol and quickly showed him how.

"O'Brien will have a man or two around the Palm, too," said Doctorow.

Bolan turned and for a moment looked at Doctorow. "If they do as good a job as they did this afternoon—"

"Hey!" Doctorow interrupted. "We're *alive!* O'Brien's guys and mine—"

"Yeah," Bolan acknowledged, but shook his head regretfully. "And let the briefcase get away. If just one or two cars had followed orders and kept on the tail of that Nissan, we'd have found out where the—"

"*Hey!* C'mon! When the Colombians opened fire, the deal was dead. You think that Nissan would have gone to the big factory, to the headquarters, after seeing a little war break out on the streets behind him? No way, buddy! When the Colombians opened fire, the operation was busted."

Bolan shrugged. "Probably right. So we're back at square one. Which is why it's important to talk to Major Thang tonight. He may want to give us some Intel. And we can sure as hell use it."

MAJOR QUANT CHANH THANG had left his wife behind in Vietnam. He had no choice about it. In the confusion of the last few days of the war, the Vietcong had overrun the suburb where they had made their home, capturing her before he could rush out there to save her. Knowing he would never see her again, he had taken a woman into his apartment to attend to his needs—as in fact she attended to hers. Tonight she frowned as she watched him shove a pistol down into the leather holster strapped under his left arm.

"It is a dangerous thing you go out to do?" she asked.

"To face one of the betrayers," said Major Thang.

"An American?"

"Of course an American! Who else betrayed us and left us to face our bitterest enemies alone? And odd, too... One of the best of the American soldiers."

She shook her head. "An old grudge in a new world," she said. "This is sad."

He concentrated on settling his leather and fixing his pistol securely in it. It was an excellent weapon for what he had to do: a Walther PPK, the little, easily hidden 7.65 mm pocket pistol developed for the German police—PPK stood for *Pistole Polizei Kriminal*. It was the perfect weapon for what he had to do. Whipped out from under his jacket at the right moment, it would fire two or three quick shots, and he could walk away before stunned witnesses would know what had happened.

Next, the major jammed his cane against the floor and stood erect. He settled a gray straw hat on his head, only half concealing the long-healed injury to his forehead, the dent made when a Cong officer had pounded him with the butt of a big military revolver.

"When I have finished this night's work," he said to his woman, "we will never again worry about money. We will leave this filthy city and live . . . we will live in Florida."

She didn't believe it, but she knew she could not talk him out of what he was going out to do. She bowed and pulled open the door.

PETE NHU SHOVED his Colt King Cobra into the big holster the weapon required. His jacket was a size too big for him— and looked odd hanging on his thin body—to make room for the .357 Magnum pistol.

"I have important business this evening," he said to Dinh My Linh. "So I will be late, probably. Maybe very late. You need not wait up for me."

The exquisitely beautiful young girl nodded mutely, then looked down on the ground.

"A major threat will be removed tonight," he added, as if by way of an explanation. He smiled, and keeping to himself thoughts he did not think she could understand, went on, "I am almost reluctant to eliminate this threat. This afternoon he all but destroyed our chief competition. The war with the Colombians is almost over. Their chief is in jail."

"That is good," she said quietly.

"It is good," he agreed. "Think of fun things to do when I come home. If you are asleep, I will wake you. We will have much to celebrate."

Mia bowed. "I will wait impatiently," she said.

AIR MARSHAL LE XUAN DIEM did not wear black leather that particular evening, nor did his girl. In their apartment, over an early dinner, they had worn black silk robes. They had eaten simply, in anticipation that later they would eat more according to their style. Now, with her assistance, the marshal dressed in a black silk suit with a white silk shirt and a black-red necktie, also of silk.

The marshal did not carry a weapon. There was risk in that. New York gun laws were unreasonably strict. Anyway, the time was long past when it was the marshal's style to swagger along the streets with a Colt .45 hanging conspicuously at his side.

Others would be armed. They would take responsibility for the firepower tonight's operation would require. He was the commanding officer, so there was no need to act as combat infantryman.

He would have soldiers on site, and they would carry his guns for him.

The scenario was not entirely simple. It involved several elements, each with an order of priority. First and foremost, someone must kill Bolan. That was Thang's assignment, but if he failed, then it became everyone else's responsibility: Pete Nhu's and Bob Lac's, to start with. If they failed—and only then—the responsibility fell to himself, Marshal Diem, and his men. They would stand aside and let others do the work and would move only if all the others failed.

Second, Major Thang. Someone had to dispose of Major Thang, and the only question was whether it should be done by Nhu or Lac. Or, of course, if it had to be, by the soldiers.

Much depended on how things worked out. Both Nhu and Lac had become too independent of late, and maybe the time had come to be rid of them. They had gained too much power since the death of the honored one.

Opportunity. It would be a night of opportunity.

BOB LAC HAD DECIDED not to eat supper. There might be time for that later—and maybe not.

He sat in a dark blue Ford van on Second Avenue. In the van with him were Ngu and Hao. All of them were armed with Heckler & Koch MP-5 assault rifles, each one fitted with a 30-round magazine. Two were the SD-3 versions, cycling subsonic rounds. These weapons were capable of far more accurate fire than the Mini-Uzi that Hao ordinarily used. Each MP-5 was capable of reliably sending a thin stream of 9 mm into a target fifty or more yards away.

Lac was rehearsing his killers.

"The American is the man who hit us last night," he said. "Sure, we want to get him. And let's do. If Thang doesn't, then we want him. But that's not the big deal. I got an idea that Marshal Diem will show up tonight. And if he does, we take him. You understand that? We take Diem."

"What about Nhu?"

Lac smiled. "Yes. But only if we get Diem first. He's the target. I want Diem."

THE PALM WAS one of the country's best steak houses. No reservations. People came and got a table if they were lucky. Sometimes customers were turned away at the door when the place was busting at the seams. But they accepted it and tried another time. The tables and chairs were rough and heavy, the walls decorated with cartoon drawings. Waiters in long white aprons hurried through, carrying big trays.

The specialty of the house was thick, juicy steak, served with heaping platters of cottage-fried potatoes and steamed vegetables. If anybody ordered wine, it came in a sizable water glass. The place was bustling, noisy, robust. Those who wanted tea and a candle on the table had to go somewhere else.

Major Thang was on time. Because he walked with a cane, he was given a table even though his guest had not yet arrived.

Bolan arrived five minutes later. He spotted the major and went over to the table. Major Thang stood, then looked at him searchingly. "Ah, the face is different," he said at last, "but nothing could change those icy eyes. . . ." He extended his hand, and the two men exchanged a hearty handshake.

"I have heard your name over the years," said Major Thang. "Some stories have come to my ears, and I have been convinced you were in the background somehow."

"I heard how you escaped," said Bolan.

"Alone," said the major sadly.

"Yes. I heard that."

The major had wanted to order wine for both of them, but only one big glass was put on the table. It was red wine, to go with steaks, and had a full satisfying taste. Bolan had decided to stick with coffee and nonalcoholic drinks. He couldn't forget he was in the midst of a war.

Major Thang began to talk about the old days, about the hard battles. He mentioned names Mack Bolan hadn't thought about for years. Food was brought, and more wine for the major. The major reminisced, and for the most part Bolan listened.

When justice had been done to his steak, the major ordered coffee and brandy and a box of cigars. Each man took a cigar, and the waiter offered lights with big wooden matches.

A TAXI PULLED UP in front of the Palm. A small young woman paid the driver before she got out, then pulled the hood of a raincoat around her face before she slipped out of the cab and hurried into the restaurant.

Inside the restaurant, she handed the raincoat over the counter to a checkroom girl.

"Table for one?"

"I meet friends," she said. "Vietnamese gentleman, and an American—"

The headwaiter pointed to where Bolan and the major sat smoking cigars. She thanked him and walked toward the table.

"Major Thang?"

The major looked up, startled. "Uh . . . yes. What can I do for you?"

"Message for thees man," she said, nodding toward Bolan. "I bring message of important."

She passed to Bolan a folded slip of paper, which she had been holding concealed in her hand since she left the taxi. It was lavender colored and tied with a ribbon.

Bolan unfolded it and read.

The man is with a gun under his coat and expects kill you when you are leaving this place. Also, a dozen or more others is outside waiting, to kill you if he fail.

Shoving the paper down into his jacket pocket, Bolan smiled at Mia and shook his head. She moved away wordlessly.

"What is it?" asked Major Thang.

"A clever new way to solicit," Bolan answered.

Major Thang smiled, cocked his head and followed the girl with his eyes. She was speaking to the headwaiter, who nodded and guided her to a table. "I might take her up on it if I were you," the major said to Bolan. "She is exceptionally pretty, and it would be a pleasant way to finish the evening."

"Perhaps," said Bolan. "Maybe I'll say good-evening to you in a few minutes and go and join her at her table."

The major frowned. "Uh . . . well . . . I really wouldn't actually. My suggestion was only a joke. She could be . . . you can't be too careful. Also, she could be the front for muggers. That's not unusual in New York, you know."

Bolan nodded thoughtfully. His abrupt retreat into his thoughts was not—as the major probably supposed—to ponder whether or not to move to the girl's table. He'd been struck by Major Thang's change of mood. The suggestion that Bolan might not leave the restaurant with him had been upsetting. His reaction had been all too plain.

Bolan concluded that Doctorow and O'Brien had been right. Apparently Major Thang had not invited him to dinner to renew an old friendship and talk about old times.

He indicated his readiness to leave, and Major Thang insisted on paying the check. He put it on an American Express card. When they were finished and had crushed out their cigars in a big glass ashtray, Bolan and the major stood and moved toward the door.

"Cab?"

"Right," said Bolan.

Yeah, a cab. A car in front of the place, to give him shelter and a chance.

"One waiting, sir." The doorman opened the door.

"After you, Major."

"After *you,* my friend," said the major with a pensive smile. "After you . . ."

Bolan seized the major's arm and steered him out the door, ahead of him.

For a moment Major Thang stood on the sidewalk, under the restaurant canopy and in a glare of light. The driver had reached back over his seat and opened the rear door of the chrome yellow New York taxi. The major glanced around, as if looking for his backup. His body was stiff, taut.

But there were other interested parties, other observers to whom the appearance of the two men was a signal. In a police van, in the Caddy across the street, in Bob Lac's van—everyone tensed. Pete Nhu stepped out of a doorway and walked slowly toward the Palm. Three others moved toward the canopy and its pool of brilliant light.

The major, smaller than Bolan, leaning on the cane in his left hand, hesitated for a moment as though he were steadying himself. Then, in a swifter movement than Bolan had anticipated, he swung around, snatching the Walther from under his jacket as he turned.

Bolan went for his Beretta. As the muzzle of the Walther came up, so did the muzzle of the Beretta. But neither man fired.

An explosion from behind drove a heavy slug into the major's chest, and he flopped back to the sidewalk, his head banging against the door of the cab.

Bolan spun around. The girl, the one who had brought him the warning, stood with her legs apart in the doorway, a black, snub-nose revolver clutched in both hands. She had fired from behind Bolan and so close that the bullet must have whipped past his right arm as he raised the Beretta.

"There is others!" she shrieked.

Damned right there were. They made themselves known with a storm of fire coming from every direction but from the restaurant.

Bolan backed through the door, nudging the girl back behind him. When both of them were inside, he kicked the door shut and grabbed the headwaiter's desk and shoved it in front of the door.

Inside the establishment the clatter of gunfire had generated panic. Diners were on the floor. Others were crowding through the back door, into the kitchen. Not just women, but men, too, screamed in fear.

When they noticed a man and woman with pistols in their hands backing into the restaurant, the panic turned to hysteria.

Bolan turned to the lovely young girl and asked, "Who are you? Why are you doing this?"

"We fight for freedom. Hmm? Call me Mia," she said.

Freedom... Sure. The word meant a lot of different things to different people. But, okay, she was risking her life. And that had to be good enough.

"I don't know who you are, Mia, or why you're here, but I have to figure we've got big trouble out there. A dozen or more, you said. So, have you got a way out of this place?"

"No, I never be here before," she said.

Bolan nodded. "Okay. We've got to find a way. If I know our friends out there on the street, they're coming in. And fast. Before the cops get here."

A WRENCH HAD BEEN thrown into the works because the police were already there. The plan had been to make the hit and get away before they showed up.

One of Nhu's men faced the door of the Palm with a Mini-Uzi and was about to empty a magazine when the roaring swarm of buckshot from a police riot gun cut him down.

Another man came out of a doorway with a grenade, pin pulled, and rolled it across the sidewalk to the door. A riot gun couldn't stop that, and the grenade exploded and blew in the door.

As people shrieked in terror, Bolan planted himself to face whoever rushed that blown-down door. A man with an Uzi did, and he fell under the impact of a single 9 mm slug from the Beretta.

Across the street in an illegally parked Cadillac limousine, Marshal Diem reached forward and slapped his driver on the shoulder. "Get us the hell out of here!" he yelled.

The driver shoved the Caddy into drive and accelerated away from the curb.

Hao screamed at Bob Lac. "Diem is scramming!"

As the Caddy sped toward the van, all three H&K MP-5 assault rifles opened on it, firing three narrow streams of 9 mm. One stream blasted in the windshield and chopped the driver and bodyguard. One stitched the front fender and tires. One blew through the side windows. The car filled with flying glass.

Marshal Diem threw himself to the floor, escaping the slugs but cut in a hundred places by glass.

The Caddy rolled against the curb a few yards past the van. Bob Lac jumped out of it and ran forward.

Marshal Le Xuan Diem looked up and for an instant was glad to see it was Lac, not a Colombian, not the Executioner. But Lac pointed the muzzle of the H&K at his face, and before the marshal could scream, a short burst of slugs shattered his head, and he landed in a bloody heap on the back-seat floor of the Caddy.

Pete Nhu understood. The cops, the narcs, had descended on the place. Maybe even the FBI! Somebody had screwed up and screwed up good. There had to be a leak somewhere. Obviously Bolan had been warned.

But he'd be damned if he'd give up. He'd soft-probed this restaurant, and he knew where Bolan had to come out, if he didn't just sit in there and wait for an army of cops to secure the area—which didn't seem likely, given the man they were after.

Nhu worked like a platoon commander. He'd lost a couple of men, but with quiet signals he moved the rest where he wanted them. There was no point in covering the front door. He moved for the back.

Bob Lac had the same idea. With Ngu and Hao, he moved up Forty-fifth Street to the passage leading to an alley behind the Palm. The garbage was collected there, and it was ready for removal in a Dumpster.

There Pete and Bob met face-to-face.

"Somebody blew the deal," said Pete Nhu. He stood there in the shadows, King Cobra in his hand, though he had not yet fired a shot. He glanced down at Bob Lac's H&K MP-5. "I see you came to do business."

"I've *done* business, my friend," said Lac. "The marshal was prepared to move in on us, betray us—"

"The Cadillac?" Nhu whispered hoarsely. "I thought that was the cops."

"We own it all now, my friend," said Lac. "Diem is dead. Thang is dead. I see no reason to worry about Colonel Cao. It's ours. We have only one threat to deal with."

Nhu glanced around, as if he could see things in the shadows. "Someone betrayed us," he said morosely. "Someone carried a warning."

Lac slapped his automatic rifle with affection and trust. "We'll worry about the traitor after we take care of the sharpshooter. He's in there. He won't go out the front."

"I want that man," said Nhu. "For sure."

MACK BOLAN HAD LED Dinh My Linh up a flight of stairs above the restaurant, into the area where the staff changed clothes. They quickly went through the waiter's locker room.

"We could walk out the front door," he said to her. "The cops are out there, and narcs. Can you afford that?"

Mia bit her lower lip. "I illegal alien," she said sadly. "I don't want go back my old country. My family not want go, either. I don't want be questioned of police."

"We can get killed trying to get out any other way," he said.

"Yes..."

"I owe it to you. But be square with me. Who are you?"

"I am slave," she said simply.

He looked at the expensive silk dress she wore and shook his head.

"I *am*. My father sold me Bui Dang Nhu, for the money that bought my family's boat and makes possible them to earn living fishing. I—"

"Who is Bui Dang Nhu?"

"The chief man in the...in the narcotic trade," she said. "He is very bad man—called Pete Nhu. He is giving much money Major Thang to murder you. He was sure it would happen."

"What did you care?" Bolan asked.

"The slave cares about freedom," she said. "And your name I had heard—as an enemy of slavery. He wishes kill you. Then he will enslave more people. To his substance."

"Sotty," said Bolan.

"*La sottisse,*" she said.

"We haven't got time to talk. It's gonna be one way or another around here, pretty damned quick."

"If you save me from police, I can help," she said.

"I owe you anyway, but how can you help?"

"I can take you place where they make the drug. Where they make *la sottisse.*"

There were not that many escape routes, and Bolan acted quickly. On a fire escape one floor above the level of the pavement, he stared down into the dark and saw the points of fire on two cigarettes.

They had to be gunmen, holding the passageway to Forty-fifth Street. But he didn't know, so he couldn't fire on them.

Mia, crouching beside him, peered into the dark, then whispered to him, "Bad men."

He touched her lips lightly to tell her to keep quiet.

Mia reached into her purse and took out a tube of lipstick. She nudged him, showed it to him and stared, inquiring.

Bolan could make out her face and understand her question. He nodded.

She tossed the lipstick. It fell on top of a garbage can with a bang and clatter.

One of the smokers let fly a short burst of automatic fire. The yellow-blue flash off his muzzle momentarily lighted the passageway, and the bullets clattered off bricks and concrete.

Bolan aimed the Beretta 93-R and squeezed off one shot. The flash hider hid the brief glare at the pistol's muzzle, and the subsonic round took out the gunman without a sound the second gunman could hear.

In fact, the other one didn't know his partner had fallen. He pressed himself against a brick wall and didn't move.

Bolan flipped a cartridge out of one of his spare clips. He gave it a little toss, and it clattered on the pavement beside the body of the dead gunman.

The gunman called out a man's name quietly, but when he heard no response, he crossed the passageway to find out what had happened. He tossed away his cigarette. It broke against a wall in a small shower of sparks, and he moved then without his identifying point of orange fire. Bolan couldn't see him.

The burst of fire the first gunman had loosed at Mia's lipstick had drawn attention from all over. A blue-and-white now came to a noisy stop at the end of the passageway and directed a spotlight back into the narrow way.

The surviving gunman sprayed 9 mm bullets, and the police spotlight went out in a little explosion.

The gunman staggered forward, charging against the NYPD car as if it were an offending animal.

From his elevated vantage point Bolan could see what happened. The wounded policeman fired from the car. A single shot from his police revolver produced a prolonged chatter from the automatic weapon. The twenty or thirty slugs from the passageway all missed the cop. The cop's second single shot did not miss.

The gunman stood and focused all his attention on his wound, but a second shot eliminated his concern, and he sprawled forward.

Mia gripped Bolan's arm and squeezed.

He turned to her. "Okay, good riddance. But not good news if we want to get out of here on our own."

They climbed higher on the fire escape. The doors opened into the third and fourth floors of the buildings. Those doors were locked, and forcing one of them would almost certainly have set off an alarm. From the top platform of the fire escape there was a steel ladder to the roof. Bolan went up the ladder and looked around.

The roof was flat. He climbed back down and offered Mia his hand, to help her onto the roof, and in a moment they were on the top. They crept to the edge and looked down on Second Avenue.

The neighborhood was alive with flashing red lights. Every few seconds another vehicle with emergency lights pulled into the block. People who had fled the restaurant milled in confusion on the sidewalk. The body of Major Thang had been covered with a plastic sheet. In the next block, all four doors of a Cadillac limousine were open. Bolan could see a bloody corpse sprawled in the back seat.

Bolan turned to Mia. "I want to go where the stuff is made," he said. "We've got to find a way out of this neighborhood."

14

Pete Nhu walked into his apartment briskly and called out, "Mia!"

He strode across the living room and opened the door to his bedroom. Then he looked in the bathroom, the kitchen. He called her name again. *"Mia!"*

Bob Lac had followed him into the apartment and stood in the middle of the living room. He cradled his H&K MP-5 under his arm and pulled out a half-empty magazine to make room for a full one. He glanced around. Hao was just outside, in the hall outside the apartment. Ngu was downstairs with two of Nhu's men, guarding the doors.

"I'm afraid we know who carried the warning," said Lac quietly.

Nhu glared at him in cold fury. But in a moment his face fell, and he nodded. "And so she dies," he muttered.

"She's with the cops," said Lac. "Which means they'll be here any minute."

"No. She isn't with the cops. She's got her problems with the cops. She's not legal in this country. None of her family is legal, so she'd be scared to talk to them. They'd ask her who she is. That was her that got out of the cab and went in, wearing a raincoat when it wasn't raining. She's with Bolan. She warned him—God knows why. And it must have been Mia who shot Major Thang. Bolan didn't. I was watching him. He didn't shoot Thang."

"She's too damned smart," Lac said.

Nhu grabbed open the center drawer in a small desk in the living room. "Too damned smart by half," he said. "I had a little Colt in here. It's gone."

"She killed Thang with it."

Nhu sighed impatiently and glanced around the apartment, as if he thought he still might find the girl lying asleep on his couch or hiding and laughing in a closet. "Whatever," he said. "I don't think the cops will be arriving any time soon. But I think Bolan will. That's the way he works, they say. So we have a chance to get him yet. All we have to do is be ready."

Lac smiled. "If we take out Bolan tonight, the city is ours."

"It won't be easy," said Nhu. "We must prepare."

The lab was in the back of the third floor, the same floor as the apartment. It operated twenty-four hours a day, and when Nhu and Lac went back there, they were met at the door by the night foreman, a man named Phat.

"We may be attacked," said Nhu. "How many men are reliable?"

Phat was a gray-haired, emaciated man. He was smoking a cigarette and he removed it from his mouth to glance around at the night crew working in the lab. "Me," he said. "And three boys. The women..." He shrugged.

"Do they know how to use guns?" Lac asked, nodding at the three men inside the lab, the ones Phat had called boys.

"Sure."

Nhu handed Phat a key. "Take them downstairs and get guns out of the supply. Heavy stuff, with plenty of ammunition."

Lac stepped into the lab. He had never seen it before, and though he knew how much sotty it turned out each week, he was surprised.

A dozen girls, maybe fifteen, were at work—all of them Vietnamese and none of them older than twenty. Most of them were busy at a table in the middle of the room, where they carefully measured cocaine and heroin from plastic buckets into plastic cups. They pressed down lids on the cups and shook them to mix the powders thoroughly. Then they measured the mixture into glass bowls.

The bowls were lined up on carts and wheeled across the room to where a man opened a little valve on a can and drew a measured amount of ether. He poured ether into each bowl, then stirred.

The man wore a respirator so he would not inhale the ether.

When ether had been stirred into the powder in each bowl on a cart, a girl wheeled the cart to a microwave oven. The mixture was cooked by microwave.

Each microwave oven stood inside a heavy wooden closet, which was closed when the oven was started. A quiet exhaust fan cleared the ether fumes from each closet. Ether was dangerously volatile, and if a dish blew up, the closet would confine the explosion.

Nhu stepped into the lab and took notice of how carefully Lac was studying the operation. "The microwaves cook the stuff fast," he said, "and with less danger of explosion."

When removed from the oven, the sotty looked like a solid disk of crystallized brown sugar. At another table, three girls were occupied with breaking the disks into little rocks of sotty. They dropped the rocks into clear plastic envelopes. Two others weighed the envelopes. They added another small rock or two, or poured out a rock or two, to make each envelope contain the right amount.

When the envelopes were prepared, they were passed on to the last worker in the chain. She shoved the open end of each envelope into a machine that sealed it with heat.

"You sell in vials," said Nhu, "your dealers will pour a rock or so out of half the vials, to make themselves two or three extra vials out of each shipment—which they sell for their own profit. You sell in sealed envelopes, they can't do that."

"You don't miss a trick, do you?" said Lac. "The honored one said that about you."

"The only trick I missed with the honored one was in letting the spics get him before I did," said Nhu bitterly. "And now, my friend, let's organize our troops. We will have to fight a battle before long."

GETTING DOWN FROM THE ROOF above the Palm had proved less difficult than Bolan had thought it might be. He had led the delicately beautiful Vietnamese girl from that roof to another, then to still another. She began to tremble with fear, not of the height or the jumps they had to make, but from the realization that she was wanted now, not just as an illegal alien but as the woman who had killed Major Thang.

Bolan had finally broken the lock on the door to stairs leading down from a roof into an apartment building, and he and Mia had walked casually down through the building, encountering on the way a couple who greeted them warmly, assuming they were leaving a noisy party that was going on in a flat on the third floor.

Twenty minutes later they were in his hotel room, well south of Forty-fifth Street.

Mia sat on his bed, watching him change his clothes—change *himself*, really, from Mack Bolan, warrior having dinner with an old veteran of one of his wars, to the Executioner. She watched him dress in black—not the black combat suit he'd rather have worn and couldn't in the streets of New York, but in black slacks, black T-shirt, black nylon jacket, with the leather that carried his weapons under the jacket.

"I am not surprised," she said.

"I knew you wouldn't be."

She watched him push extra magazines down into the pockets on his harness, which also held a knife, a light, three grenades.

"I did destroy what gives me life," she said. "If you kill Bui Dang Nhu, I am poor girl, no citizen, no home. If he kill you, he kill me."

Bolan stopped what he was doing and stared hard at her. He nodded. "I'll arrange a new life for you."

"You can do this thing? I be thankful."

"All right." He sat down at the hotel-room desk and wrote a note with the ballpoint pen the hotel provided.

Hal Brognola
Special Operations Group
Department of Justice
Hal—
Take care of this girl. She has served us well. If I don't make it, take care of her. For me. Favor.

Striker

"That man's in Washington," he said to her. "Show him this note. Trust him."

Mia stared at the note, then looked up at him. "Thank you," she breathed.

"Now. Where's the lab? Where is Pete Nhu?"

WHITE STREET. He had to make a very quick, incomplete recon. He just had a cab drive him through. If Nhu was smart, his defense would begin on the street. He'd have wiseguys out, watching for a probe. If he was really smart, those guys wouldn't make a move, just give Nhu the signal.

Bolan had made many quick recons before. He knew how to get a lot of Intel out of one short look.

The street was mostly dark. Lights shone in some windows. People lived in apartments in two or three of these buildings. In other windows Bolan could see the stark dim glow of safety lights—including dim gray light in the windows of the Nhu Carpet Cleaning Company.

It was a very ordinary city street, in an older neighborhood—a street of four-and five-story brick buildings in various states of repair, all of them jammed against each other. Some had been well restored with sandblasting. One looked vacant. Another one was in the process of being restored.

That could be useful. The house adjoined the address the girl had given him. A huge Dumpster sat on the curb, filled with plaster and lath—the debris that had been hauled out of the building. The Dumpster, too, might be useful.

Then he spotted the wiseguys—two of them, maybe three. But not terribly smart. If Nhu and these legbreakers were *really* smart, they'd have been positioned where they wouldn't be seen. Problem with guys like these was that they always had the idea they were so tough that anyone who saw them would be scared off, so they swaggered and glared and dared somebody to come near them.

So that was the setup. Legbreakers on the street, and inside the building there had to be a dozen, maybe twenty, and they'd be packing heavy iron, for sure.

Around the corner on Broadway, Bolan told the cabbie to pull to the curb. "Listen," he said. "The meter's three-fifty. Here's twenty bucks, and here's what I want you to do. Go around and come out into White Street again, from the west end. Come through slow, like you're looking for an address. When we get to that Dumpster, I'm probably going to jump out—depending on whether certain guys are looking. Just drive on. Keep moving, same speed. Don't look back, don't come back."

"Ya got it," said the cabbie, taking the twenty-dollar bill. "How 'bout we sit here a few minutes, so it don't look like the same cab comes back too soon?"

"Good idea."

The cab driver sat staring out through his windshield, making a point of not looking back at his passenger. "You a cop?" he asked.

"Not exactly."

The cabbie pondered that answer for a while, then said, "Somethin' must be comin' down back there. I don't want to know what. But I never heard of nothin' on White Street."

"Neither did I, till tonight."

After a few more minutes, the driver moved on up Broadway, made his turns and came back to White Street the way Bolan had told him. He drove slowly, gawking around, making a show of looking for a number.

Bolan had already opened the door and held it cracked so he could jump out when he wanted to. He stared at the sidewalks on both sides. The legbreakers were still where he'd seen them before, one on each side of the street. He didn't spot a third one. Maybe there wasn't a third one.

They passed the legbreakers and the building the girl had said was Nhu's. The driver edged a cab close to the Dumpster. Just short of it, Bolan jumped out, giving the door a little push, not slamming it, but not leaving it hang open, either. He caught his balance. He was against the Dumpster and in its shadow, and no one was moving against him.

Not yet, anyway.

He drew his Beretta from its leather to have the silenced pistol at the ready in case he needed it, and he crouched in the shadow and waited for a reaction from the street.

Nothing. If one of the legbreakers had seen him jump from the cab, he was smart enough only to signal somebody else and not to move. But Bolan doubted those two legbreakers were that smart.

Moving slowly and quietly, he brought himself around to where he could study the door of the building being remodeled. The door was gone, leaving the interior open to the streets. The remodeling crew must have figured there was nothing inside to steal, no reason to try to keep the place locked up—which would have been useless anyway since all the windows were out.

As the warrior studied the legbreakers, a car came through the street. The sentries stared, and Bolan knew that he'd have to take advantage of such a favorable distraction to make his move.

A little luck came his way when two vehicles came at once, a car and a van, both entering the street from Broadway.

Bolan slipped around the Dumpster and trotted up the littered stone steps of the building and through the open door into its dark and dusty interior.

He went to a window, his feet crunching on broken plaster and scattered lath. The legbreakers were still where they had been. They showed no sign of having seen him make his move.

Bolan began a recon of the building.

Except for where a little street light came in through the door or a window, the place was dark and stank of plaster dust and mould and decay. They were taking out all the interior walls, even replacing much of the studding. The wiring and plumbing had been already stripped out.

The remodelers had exposed the brick wall that separated the building from Nhu's next door. He moved back toward the rear of the building and then knelt and shone his light on a section of old bricks.

The bricks were pink and soft, maybe a hundred years old. The mortar was rotten. The wall was not load bearing, fortunately; the weight of the building was carried by steel beams that were also exposed.

The warrior withdrew his Puuko knife from its sheath on his combat harness. With its tip he tested the mortar between two bricks. It yielded to the carbon steel.

So maybe here was how he could get into Nhu's lab.

Mia had briefed him about the layout of the building. The first floor, she'd said, was where Nhu did run a carpet-cleaning business. On the second floor he housed the Vietnamese girls who worked in his lab. Also, she thought he kept a cache of weapons there. On the third floor...the lab, plus the apartment where she and Nhu lived.

There was no fourth floor.

He'd check the third floor and see if he could break through into that apartment.

BUI DANG NHU and Ngo Ba Lac conferred nervously in the first-floor office of the carpet-cleaning company. They had switched off the night-lights so they could stand in the dark and stare at the street.

"I have a feeling he's got past those two men," said Lac.

"So do I, but he's not in the building. Dammit. He's not in the building! How could he? We got the doors covered front and back. We got guys on the roof, guys in the cellar, guys in every room that's got a window."

"Down the chimney like Santa Claus," Lac suggested.

"It's just possible he's not coming," said Nhu.

"You don't know the man," Lac argued. "My operation was a hell of a lot smaller—which should have made it easier to protect. And not only did he find it—he took it out last night, all by himself. And it *was* protected. I had a security system. Giap was there, with half a dozen tough guys. Plus two more upstairs. *One man,* Pete. Just one goddamn man!"

"So whatta we do? You got any ideas?" Nhu asked irritably.

"We move around this place," said Lac. "Check every man, any of them not doing his job, we motivate him. My guys got trapped in the cellar. That's what happened to them. We *move*. We keep our guys spread out. Let's check every window, every door. Let's move."

THE REMODELERS WEREN'T careful about their tools. They didn't leave expensive electric drills and saws around, but they left hammers and screwdrivers and handsaws...and crowbars that had been used to rip out walls and ceiling. When quitting time came, the tools were left there.

The warrior had picked up two crowbars and settled down on the dusty floor on the third floor, front of the building, and with his Puuko knife he began to chip out mortar.

He worked quietly. He had really no idea what was on the other side of the wall. She had said an apartment, but what room would he break into if he went through the wall? If he could remove just one brick . . .

He tapped the knife handle with one of the crowbars, driving the carbon-steel tip into the crumbly mortar. He twisted. The soft old mortar broke, and he could shove chips of it away.

In a couple of minutes he had enough mortar dug out to let him push the tip of a crowbar between two bricks. He wedged the crowbar then tried twisting it. The bricks moved a little, cracking mortar and making it easier to remove. He used the knife to dig out more.

It took a little time and sweat, but in a few more minutes he had a brick loose. The crowbar helped him pry it out. He shone his light into the hole.

Great! All he could see was another brick. The wall was a party wall, but it was not just one brick thick.

He'd come this far. Wedging the crowbar in the hole, he pried out another brick, then another one. Each time he pried a brick loose and made the hole bigger, he made it easier to break more bricks loose. The mortar readily gave way to the force he could exert with the crook in the crowbar. In less time than he'd needed to remove the first brick, he pried off twenty-five or thirty more.

And the only thing facing him was another wall.

It was just like the one he'd broken through—soft old bricks, crumbling mortar. So he started to work again, and in a few minutes he had loosened one brick and could pull it out.

What he saw next was lath and plaster.

He put the point of the Puuko knife between two strips of lath and twisted it like a drill, cutting a hole through the plaster. Again he worked quietly, slowly. In half a minute, even so, the point of the knife cut through.

He pulled the blade back. He could see light.

He had switched off his own light, and he sat on the floor in the dark and listened for a reaction from the other side of the plaster. When he heard nothing, he pushed the knife into the hole and enlarged it.

Now he could put his eye up to the hole and look.

A bedroom.

She had not described it, but he had no doubt it was the room where she had slept with Nhu. It was a big room, with green carpeting and drapes, and he could see a green spread on the bed. A lamp burned on a bedside table, and the room was filled with restful yellowish light.

The warrior held his eye to the hole and watched for several minutes. He saw no one.

He continued his labors with the bricks again, this time working more quietly. In maybe ten minutes he had a hole big enough to crawl through.

Now he set to work on the lath. With the knife he cut it away, piece by piece. He didn't crack it; he cut it. He didn't want to make noise, and he didn't want the plaster wall to fall before he was ready.

When he had cut away the lath, he began to enlarge his peephole. Every few seconds he stopped to look and listen.

Shortly he had a hole big enough to put his head through. Very slowly, he carefully thrust his head into the room and looked around. The bedroom was in fact deserted.

He started to cut quickly. In three or four more minutes he crawled through and stood up inside the bedroom of Bui Dang Nhu's apartment.

The floor inside the hole he had just made was littered with plaster dust, and he was trying to decide whether he should quietly close the bedroom door or switch off the lamp. As he looked around, a door opened somewhere in the apartment, and he heard the voices of Nhu and Lac.

"If I ever get my hands on that little bitch, she's gonna die a slow and painful death," said one man.

"Yeah. Can't let her get away with it," came the response.

"Brandy?"

"Make it Scotch."

Bolan had no doubt about who they were. The Beretta 93-R was in his hand. With its suppressor in place and cycling subsonic rounds, it could take out the two Vietnamese drug kingpins in seconds. They wouldn't know what hit them, and their wiseguys wouldn't know they were gone.

But if they kept talking, maybe they'd tell him something about how their security was laid out.

He waited and listened.

"I've been thinking of something, Bob."

"Yeah?"

"Okay. Hao and Ngu got out of your place last night, when nobody else did. Does that give you any kind of a problem? I mean, does it seem funny to you that Giap and all the other guys got it, but that pair went out an upstairs window without a scratch?"

"Listen...those guys hit the Russians for me yesterday afternoon. They took out two of the spics that tried to hit them later. And tonight they helped me get rid of Marshal Diem. If they weren't absolutely loyal—"

"Okay. Can't blame me for wondering."

"They'll hold up their end of the game tonight. Let's hope your guys do as well. Wanna make a little bet that it's those two who'll take out Bolan—if he shows?"

"Let's get downstairs and find out what they're doing."

It was handy for Bolan to know that the two Vietnamese he'd seen at work yesterday were in the building. He remembered them well. Stone killers, sure, but smart and quick, too. Downstairs.

The door slammed. The two kingpins had left the apartment, maybe carrying their drinks with them.

Anyway, he'd heard some useful Intel. They expected him. And they had the two dangerous men they called Hao and Ngu. He was glad he knew that. Those two weren't any ordinary legbreakers.

He left the bedroom and walked out into the living room of a handsome, comfortable apartment.

15

Doc Doctorow sat on Bolan's bed in his hotel room and stared at Dinh My Linh, who sat in a chair and wept.

"You are *not* under arrest," he said to her.

"If he die, I die," she sobbed. "If he no die, I sent back to where I die of shame and bitter. No hope."

Doctorow looked again at her note to Hal Brognola. "I'd say this gives you a lot of hope," he said.

"Never see this Washington man. Go to jail," she said.

The wound in Doctorow's shoulder throbbed. It was difficult for him to be patient. He had come to this hotel, knowing he would not find Bolan here but hoping. Instead he had found the girl.

She knew where Bolan had gone, but she wouldn't say.

So Doctorow did something he'd been instructed never to do. He placed a call to Hal Brognola at home in Virginia. He had to dial extra numbers to put in the code that would ring the special line.

"Pizza. We're closed."

"Doctorow."

"Oh . . . yeah. Okay."

"I want to read you a note. It says, 'Take care of this girl. She has served us well. If I don't make it, take care of her. For me. Favor.' Signed 'Striker.' She's Vietnamese. She's an illegal alien. She saved the big guy's life tonight, maybe. She needs help. Will you talk to her?"

"Put her on."

Before Doctorow handed Mia the telephone, he said to her, "Listen. You haven't heard me use the name of the man that note is addressed to. Right? So if he calls himself by that name, that *is* his name. Right?"

She thought about that for a moment, then nodded.

He gave her the telephone.

"Hello? Is that Washington?"

"This is Harold Brognola, chief of Special Operations Group, United States Department of Justice. Give me the name of the man who wrote that note."

"Bolan. In Vietnam, he was Sergeant Bolan."

"Okay. Good enough. You're under the protection of Special Operations Group. I'll send someone to bring you to Washington. You won't be harmed. Okay?"

"Okay. . ." she said skeptically.

"Let me talk to Doctorow."

She handed over the telephone.

"What do you need, Doctorow?"

"Tell her to tell me where Bolan is."

"Give her the phone again."

When the reassurance finally worked a minute later, Doctorow could call O'Brien. After that he got in touch with his own office. He had an address to pass on.

BOLAN DID A QUICK RECON. Except for the door from the living room there was no other entry to the apartment. The living room had windows—and a three-story drop to the street. The bedroom, bathroom and tiny kitchen had no windows. The hole through the bedroom wall was his retreat if he had to have one.

He went to the living room and listened. Everything beyond seemed silent.

Standing back, he reached out and turned the knob, and when nothing happened, he shoved the door open with the muzzle of the Beretta.

The hall outside apparently ran the length of the building, north-south, with a single window at each end. Look-

ing to his left, Bolan saw the ornate newel posts at the top
of a broad old stairway coming up from the floors below.
He could see that the apartment occupied the northeast
quarter of the floor. There was as much space beyond the
stairs. Across the hall two doors opened into what could be
two more apartments.

Or behind those doors there could be something else.

He heard footsteps on the stairway and stepped back into
the apartment, pulling the door but not closing it. Through
the crack he could see outside into the hall.

The man—a short, compact Vietnamese carrying a Beretta Model 12 submachine gun with a 40-round magazine
hanging awkwardly out of the bottom—strode quickly toward the far end of the hall, shoved open the door on the
southwest end and went into a room there, leaving the door
open.

It was the lab. Through the open door Bolan saw enough
to know he was looking at the best-equipped crack or sotty
lab he had ever seen. It was lighted by banks of fluorescent
tubes, and he could hear a low hum that had to be exhaust
fans taking out the ether fumes. He could see four or five
girls working. They all looked young.

Yeah. Not innocent, and yet— Well, he couldn't take out
this lab by rolling a couple of grenades in. Those girls were
doing something illegal, but they didn't deserve to die.

The man with the Beretta 12 stalked out of the lab as if he
were irritated about something. He slammed the door and
marched toward the stairway, but just at the top of the stairs
he halted. He'd noticed that the apartment door was open,
and in three quick strides he was at the door, gave it a kick
and lunged into the living room. He swung the muzzle of his
submachine gun around the room, ready to fire.

He saw Bolan a split second before a 9 mm slug from Bolan's Beretta cracked into his forehead. He stumbled forward one step and fell on Nhu's living-room carpet, staining
it with blood.

The silent round attracted no attention. Bolan stepped out into the hall and closed the apartment door.

He rushed to the stairway.

As he eyed the stairs, he wondered whether the guy he'd just taken out was the only legbreaker on the third floor. Could he be up here alone, except for the lab girls?

Anyway, if Nhu and his gang wanted to come up here, they'd come up this way. Wouldn't they? Was there any other way? Wasn't it a good place to take a stand and confront them one at a time as they came up?

He backed up and checked the door opposite the door to the apartment. It opened onto a big dark room.

Because of the darkness he didn't see that a stairway to the roof was located in the northwest corner of that room.

Okay. He could wait. He crouched on the floor and waited for somebody to come up from downstairs.

On the second floor, at a window in the dormitory where a dozen Vietnamese girls slept, Nhu and Lac stared at the street.

"The son of a bitch is too smart to show himself on the street," said Lac. "But where is Vien?"

"Somebody had better damned well go up and find out," said Nhu.

Two of the men went up to find out. They charged up the stairs, one waving a revolver, the other carrying an Uzi.

They saw Bolan a second after he spotted them—five or ten seconds after had been alerted by their boots on the stairs. The one with the revolver fell with a slug in his chest. A second slug from the subsonic-cycling Beretta tore through the throat of the man with the Uzi.

Both men lay on the upper steps of the wide stairway, dead from silent shots. And the men below would know that something was definitely up. Three of their own had gone upstairs and hadn't returned. Okay, they knew. Three guys. They had to know he was at the top of the stairs.

What had they done the night before? Blown the damned floor out, putting the automatic fire up through plaster and wood. They'd do the same again, so standing there wasn't a good idea.

Bolan trotted back into Nhu's apartment. The kitchen was straight through the door, and the living room to the left. To the right was the bath and bedroom.

He returned to the bedroom, where the hole he had made offered him a retreat if he needed it.

But not yet.

Knowing the layout of the building now, he knew the stairwell from the floors below was on the south wall of the bedroom. He grabbed a crowbar from the hole through the bricks. On the south wall, he hit the plaster with all his might. He repeated the blows, and in less than a minute he had beaten a hole from the bedroom to the stairwell. He put his ear to that hole.

Coming up. Man, they were coming up—legbreakers, wiseguys, charging recklessly up those stairs, confident that their concentrated firepower would take out the guy in the hall on the third floor.

He'd brought three MU-50-G grenades. He couldn't toss them into the lab with all those Vietnamese girls, but he could use one now. He activated it and pushed it through his hole in the wall.

The grenade went off in the stairwell, filling the air with deadly pellets.

The warrior would never know how many guys—every one of them a man determined to kill him—died in that storm of pellets. He knew one thing: that the odds, until now much against him, were even at least. And what was more, Nhu understood now that he was fighting death.

Bolan ran back to the door from the apartment.

He found about what he'd expected. The lab was defended by its own legbreakers. Two of them were in the door, holding H&K MP-5s leveled on the hall. Behind them the girls shrieked in fear.

The wiseguys with the heavy iron had no idea where the threat came from. All they heard was the explosion of the grenade. They stood in the south hall, their heavy guns ready for any target they saw.

They were not looking for an enemy in the door to Nhu's apartment.

But the enemy was looking for them.

He had replaced the clip in the Beretta, then shoved it into its leather. Now was the time for the .44 Magnum Desert Eagle. Now was the time for thunderous blasts, no longer for silent shots from the Beretta.

The warrior knelt to the side of the door of the apartment and steadied the Eagle on the two legbreakers at the door of the lab.

He was taken by surprise when a stream of 9 mm chopped the body of the dead Vietnamese lying on the floor. The fire had not come from the legbreakers at the door of the lab. This had come from directly across the hall, from the door of the dark, vacant room across the hall. A nervous gunman had thrown open that door and fired a quick burst at the only human form he saw.

Bolan couldn't know it, but one of the legbreakers on the roof had come down when he heard the exploding grenade.

The Executioner was between two lines of fire.

He threw himself to the floor and rolled over, back into the apartment, coming up with the Eagle ready to fire back at the door across the hall.

He didn't need to see his target. He knew where it was. He loosed a shot from the big automatic, through the wall of the apartment.

The .44 Magnum slug blew out a basketball-sized hole in the wall between the apartment and the hall and another in the opposite wall. He fired again through a cloud of plaster dust.

The guy across the hall yelled in pain and shock.

Girls from the lab ran shrieking toward the stairway. Two bodies lay on the stairs, one of top of the Uzi he'd been carrying when he was stopped by Bolan's 9 mm slug. The girls jumped over the bodies. Two of them fell. A knot of them formed at the top of the stairs, shoving and elbowing each other in their panic and their fury to escape.

Bolan could not fire in the hall—not with those girls between him and the two wiseguys with the heavy iron. They had H&K MP-5s—as dangerous weapons as a man could carry, but he could not fire on them. He put another .44 Magnum slug through the door of the room across the hall for good measure, to discourage another hardman lurking in that darkness.

NHU WAS YELLING at Lac. *"I told you!* I warned you! The man is a devil! We are fighting a phantom!"

"It is—"

"You *doubt* who it is?"

"Your men! Hao and Ngu. Get them into action some way. Not up those stairs, but around behind him. Goddamn their play guns! The toughest! Give them the best we have!"

Lac smiled at Nhu. "You give orders, boss?" he asked.

Nhu, breathing hard, frowned at Lac. He understood. "No. Partners. *Equal* partners. What you want? Senior partner? I kill you first. Equal partners, my friend. The way it was on our knees before Vgo Nguyen Minh. Equal... What do you say, partner?"

Lac yelled. "Hao! Ngu! Last night's man is up there! Your chance!"

BOLAN'S PROBLEM WAS the two hardmen from the lab. Plus anybody in the darkness across the hall.

The two guys from the lab had tough weapons. Bolan had seen that. Question was, did they know how to use them? Not every man was good with a weapon like an H&K MP-

5. For himself, it was one of his favorites. For a dumb leg-breaker, it might be more gun than he could handle.

A lot of guys turned hard weapons on people who couldn't oppose them, citizens with no weapons at all—which was usual—or citizens with popguns. They usually thought they were big men when they won battles where all the odds were with them. They thought they were tough. That was one of the advantages used by a man like the Executioner—to bring combat skills against armed bullies.

Combat skills meant a guy who knew what counted when real men faced real men. It was easier, and always had been, when real men faced criminal bullies.

The bullies didn't plan on that. They didn't figure on anybody really fighting back.

But some people did. Some people drove the crack dealers off their blocks. Using some of the same tactics employed by the Executioner. Some people faced the fury, took their casualties and won.

Some did. And some died. But for most people, the terror was too much to face.

Tonight, in his hole, the Executioner faced everything a man stood against. And he meant to win.

He edged his way to the door to have a look down the hall. A burst of 9 mm splintered the door frame and drove him back.

He trotted into the bedroom. He couldn't shove another grenade through his hole in the wall because shrieking girls were still jostling on the stairs. But he could see through that hole, and he could fire through it.

Another burst smashed through the door and wall in the living room. One wiseguy was covering the other, trying to drive the warrior back while the other advanced along the hall.

But Bolan wasn't behind that door. Not now. Through the hole in the bedroom wall he could see the wiseguy working his way along the hall, MP-5 up and ready to fire. He wasn't Vietnamese. He was a big man with a beard.

The Executioner fired through the hole. The .44 Magnum slug tore through the man's ribs and out the back, destroying everything in him that counted.

The other wiseguy with an MP-5 loosed a long burst down the hall—a useless burst of fire, a nervous reaction, and a big mistake, since some of the slugs blew out the window at the end of the hall and flew across the street and into another building. That would bring the police for sure, if the sounds of firing in here hadn't already produced a call to 911.

It was a mistake in another way, too, since that long burst had emptied the magazine on the MP-5 and left the wiseguy with a dead gun.

Bolan figured it was time to get out of the apartment, which was becoming a trap. He went back to the living room and edged over to the shattered door. He looked down the hall. The wiseguy with the MP-5 had run back into the lab apparently, probably to get more ammo.

The warrior kicked open the door to the dark room on the other side of the hall. In the light that went in from the hall he could see the man who had fired at him. The guy sat against the wall, clutching his leg, trying to stop the flow of blood. His submachine gun, a Beretta 12, lay where he had dropped it. Bolan picked it up, pulled out the magazine and ejected the round from the chamber.

But now he knew there were stairs to the roof. That was where the guy had come from; he'd been the guard up there. The room was a storeroom. Bolan could see cans of ether and boxes that probably contained heroin and cocaine.

At the other end of the room there was a door, obviously opening into the lab.

It was time to work with the silenced Beretta again. They didn't know where he was, and there was no point in letting them know. The Executioner switched pistols.

He went to the door and risked a look down the hall.

The wiseguy had put a new magazine in his MP-5 and was in the hall, cautiously edging along the wall toward the apartment.

Bolan went into the lab. It was deserted. He crossed it and came out behind the wiseguy. A quick, quiet shot from the Beretta took care of him.

BOTH ENDS OF WHITE STREET were closed by police cars. An NYPD task force, under the command of Captain O'Brien, was saturating the neighborhood. They were doing it quietly.

Doctorow sat in the command car with O'Brien. Natalie stood beside it. They had heard bursts of fire from inside the building with the sign that said Nhu Carpet Cleaning Company. Right now it was quiet.

"One man . . ." Natalie said thoughtfully.

"We can't go in," said O'Brien. "Not till we know where he is and what's coming down in there."

"If only the guy weren't so damned independent," muttered Doctorow.

O'Brien shook his head. "I've got it figured out who he is. Being independent is what makes him so effective. Even so, I wish we could help him."

THE WARRIOR WAS in the middle of the hall. He was in possession of the third floor.

He heard a rising screaming, accompanied by what sounded like weeping and pleading. Girls. Screaming, weeping, pleading. They were on the stairs, from the sound of it. He edged forward to where he could get a look.

Three young Vietnamese girls were chained on the stairs. One of the tough guys he had seen kill the Russians was snapping on the last handcuff as Bolan got his look. Two were handcuffed to the bannisters. One was handcuffed between them. They made a steel-and-human chain across the stairway.

The tough guy backed away from the girls, leaving just one man below and behind them, with an H&K MP-5 in his hands.

Bolan got the idea. He couldn't go down the stairs. The guy with the MP-5 could shove his muzzle between two girls and fire up; but Bolan could not fire at him—or *would* not, since he wouldn't take the real risk of hitting one of the girls.

The warrior had possession of the third floor, but as far as the enemy knew, he couldn't go down.

They didn't know about the hole in the bedroom wall.

NHU AND LAC WERE on the roof with the stone killer called Ngu, and all three of them had MP-5s.

They had gone out the back door of the building and in the back door of the building next door. Like Bolan they had climbed up through the dust and rubble of the remodeling, but they had not seen the hole he had made leading into the apartment. This building had four floors, and they had gone all the way to the top, out onto the roof, and had dropped to the roof of the lab building.

Maybe the man below had found the way to the roof, and maybe he hadn't. Anyway, he wasn't up here, and Bob Lac had made a plan for getting him.

It was no longer a matter of saving the lab. They were surprised the cops weren't here already.

What they had to do was save themselves. But first they had to kill Bolan. They'd never get another chance like this. Besides, they had to figure that after tonight he'd be on their case forever, until sooner or later he got to them. There was no surviving, no rebuilding the business, with that man alive.

Besides . . . he'd made them mad. All of them—all who were still alive. Just five of them. Nhu and Lac. Ngu and Hao, and Phat, the lab manager, who was on the stairs behind the girls, keeping Bolan on the third floor.

If he tried to come up, they'd get him on the narrow stairs or at the hatch that opened onto the roof. If he didn't, they would drop a grenade into the storeroom below and charge down into the smoke and confusion.

Hao had finished chaining the girls across the stairway and was on his way up. Let Bolan face five men armed with the toughest guns money could buy. Lac, who had made the plan, wasn't sure what would suit him best—for Bolan to try to come up or for him to stay down there and wait for them.

THE EXECUTIONER UNDERSTOOD what the enemy had in mind, and he had no intention of doing either. They could have only two possible reasons for trying to barricade him on the third floor. Either they meant to escape from the building while he was stuck up there, or they would come down from the roof.

He didn't think much of the idea that they would try to escape. They'd had their chance to do that but had sent guys up to get him. No. They wanted him. He'd given them reasons.

He crossed the top of the stairway. The legbreaker behind the chained girls saw him but didn't have time to move.

Bolan returned to the bedroom and went through his hole, back into the torn-out building.

He went for the stairs, but in a moment he knew he was not alone. His own feet crunched broken plaster, but someone coming up the stairs was crunching heavier, noisier.

Then stopped. Whoever it was had heard him above and had stopped.

Bolan stood still where the stairs reached the third floor, silently waiting in the dark. Bolan leathered the Desert Eagle and drew the Beretta 93-R. This was a test of nerves, and a silent weapon tested tougher.

Bolan heard the man on the stairs take one cautious step. Maybe the man wasn't sure of what he'd heard. Maybe he thought he'd heard a rat.

Bolan stared into the darkness of the stairwell. He could not see so much as the shadow of the man. It would have been easy to fire a shot down the stairs, but he couldn't be sure who was coming up. It could even prove to be the police. But it wasn't likely.

The man took one more step.

Suddenly the darkness was split by the angry blue-yellow fire from the muzzle of an automatic weapon. The man on the stairs had climbed high enough to shove the muzzle through the balusters of the stairs, and he loosed a burst that tore through the room, narrowly missing Bolan, just to the right.

In an instant that muzzle would swing over for the next burst. But there wouldn't be a next burst. The Executioner knew now that he was facing a legbreaker, not a cop, and what was more, he knew where to return fire.

The Beretta spit a silent slug, and the man fell back, in his dying spasm triggering the submachine gun and letting loose a stream of 9 mm.

"HAO!" yelled Ngu.

"Two bursts," said Nhu. "Maybe he found him. Maybe he got him."

Lac shook his head. "That's in the other building," he said. "What could Hao have been shooting at in there?"

"Nerves," said Nhu.

"Not him," muttered Lac. He glanced up at the roof of the other building, one floor above them. "If Bolan gets up there, he can shoot down on us. We've gotta get off this roof. Now!"

The three of them—Lac, Nhu and Ngu—raced for the trapdoor and the narrow stairs down to the storeroom and the lab. Lac reached the trapdoor first. He jerked it open and dropped a grenade into the storeroom below.

Before the explosion they heard a scream, the anguished scream of their own man who lay wounded in the storeroom.

"Who the hell was that?" Lac yelled. "Maybe we got him after all!"

THE WARRIOR HEARD the explosion. He was pushing through the hole in the wall and back into the bedroom of the apartment. He'd figured the wiseguys wouldn't stay on the roof after they heard firing in the building next door. He had understood the situation exactly the same way Lac had understood it.

They had heavy stuff, but so did he.

He drew the Desert Eagle.

The door to the storeroom had been blown off. The grenade had made almost no smoke but had peppered the walls with pellets, breaking plaster and filling the storeroom with dust. The three men from the roof ran for the door and the hallway, coughing from the choking dust.

The first man through the door was Lac. He saw Bolan in the door of the apartment and raised the muzzle of his MP-5. A .44 Magnum slug blew his head apart.

Nhu stumbled over Lac. He pulled his trigger, and the storm of fire from his MP-5 ripped the floor as he jerked the muzzle upward. Bolan's second shot punched into his abdomen and knocked him sprawling on his back.

Ngu was a killer by instinct, experience and preference. He had let the two younger men run recklessly ahead. Now he aimed his MP-5 toward the door and fired a short, controlled burst. Then he fired another, through the wall of the storeroom, across the hall and through the wall of the living room of the apartment. A few slugs were stopped by studs, but most of them chopped through and exploded in a shower of plaster just above Bolan's head.

He had thrown himself to the floor. He lay still, figuring the man across the hall would not fire a second burst at the same place. He was right. The next burst blasted through on the other side of the door and clattered into the refrigerator and stove in the kitchen.

The warrior knew automatic weapons. He knew those three bursts would empty the magazine of all but the few submachineguns that carried bigger ones. He could take a chance that this was not one of those few.

He rose on his knees and fired .44 Magnum slugs through the walls. Only he fired low. His fire would not pass over a man prone on the floor.

He emptied the clip, and the pistol stayed open, ready for another clip. He attached a loaded clip—eight more shots—and shoved a cartridge into the chamber. As he reloaded, he moved, dashing from the living room into the bedroom, where at least part of the walls remained intact.

A stream of 9 mm followed him. The bathroom was between the bedroom and the hall, and the steel of the fixtures stopped most of the slugs—the lower ones especially, which hit the bathtub.

Bolan looked out through the hole he had earlier punched in the bedroom wall. The handcuffed girls screamed—except for one, who had fainted. The thin gray man who was sheltering behind the girls kept his station, grimly puffing on a cigarette.

The one across the hall was dangerous. Bolan much doubted if the man cared about the girls chained on the stairs. If he killed them, or some of them, it wouldn't bother him.

A burst of 9 mm blasted through the bathroom and bedroom walls—most of the slugs stopped, but a few punched out in a cloud of plaster.

And that was the end for the gunman across the hall. He had been firing through two walls, but not where Bolan could see both walls. This burst broke through the bathroom wall and the bedroom wall, and Bolan, watching through the bathroom door, could see the angle. He could trace the line back and could tell exactly where the burst had come from.

He took aim with the Eagle and loosed four shots that went almost through the same holes that last blast of 9 mm had made—only in the opposite direction. He heard the gunman grunt and stumble. He heard a final short burst of submachine gun fire—heard it but saw nothing of it. It had been fired by the falling gunner's last convulsive tug on the trigger, and the slugs went through the ceiling.

PHAT RETREATED, and running out onto White Street he all but ran into the arms of a dozen of New York's finest.

Doctorow, Natalie and Captain O'Brien ran up the stairs, through a swarm of shrieking Vietnamese girls. When they reached Bolan, he was kneeling beside the terrified handcuffed girls, trying to assure them that the danger was over and that they would be released in a few minutes.

Searching through the bullet-shattered wreckage of Nhu's apartment, they found more than two and half million dollars in cash.

Bolan counted off fifty thousand dollar bills. As Doctorow and O'Brien watched curiously, he stuffed the money in a big brown envelope he had found in Nhu's desk. He handed the envelope to Doctorow.

"What's this?" asked the surprised narcotics agent.

"For the young woman," said Bolan. "He owed her. Besides, she'll need it to get started in a new life."

"Fine with me," said O'Brien. "I didn't see anybody put any money in any envelope. That is, if anybody asks."

Doctorow handed the envelope back to Bolan. "What envelope?" he asked. "I didn't see any envelope. Anyway, you'll have to hand it to her yourself, big guy. Hal called back. He said you should bring Dinh My Linh to Washington yourself—if you didn't get yourself killed tonight. He needs to talk to you. Something stirring in the Far East he thinks will interest you. You speak Japanese?"

"Do the Japanese speak English?" Bolan asked wryly.

"He said to tell you a Lear jet would be waiting for you at Teterboro Airport and you should get the girl on it and come to Washington tonight if you can."

A few minutes later Mack Bolan left the building on White Street with Doc Doctorow and Captain O'Brien.

As they walked along the street toward the NYPD car that would take them to Bolan's hotel and then to Teterboro, one of the officers guarding the end of the street turned to his partner and asked, "Who's the big fellow?"

The other officer shrugged. "Another narc, I guess. Another Fed."

"Don't think so," said the first officer. "I think he's somethin' special. Some special kind of guy."

THE MEDELLÍN TRILOGY

THE EXECUTIONER

Message to Medellín: The Executioner and his warriors are primed for the biggest showdown in the cocaine wars—and are determined to win!

Don't miss The Medellín Trilogy—a three-book action drama that pits THE EXECUTIONER, PHOENIX FORCE and ABLE TEAM against the biggest narco barons and cocaine cowboys in South America. The cocaine crackdown begins in May in THE EXECUTIONER #149: *Blood Rules,* continues in June in the longer 352-page Mack Bolan novel *Evil Kingdom* and concludes in July in THE EXECUTIONER #151: *Message to Medellín.*

Look for the special banner on each explosive book in The Medellín Trilogy and make sure you don't miss an episode of this awesome new battle in The Executioner's everlasting war!

Take
4 explosive books
plus a
mystery bonus
FREE

In the Deathlands,
everyone and everything is fair game,
but only the strongest survive....

JAMES AXLER

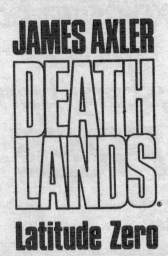

DEATH LANDS®

Latitude Zero

Heading west toward the nearest gateway, Ryan Cawdor and his band of post-holocaust survivors are trapped in a nightmare when a deal necessary for their survival pits them against Ryan's oldest enemy—a sadistic, ruthless man who would stop at nothing to get his hands on Ryan Cawdor.